**She'd Never Wanted To Get Involved
With Another Roth Again, But It
Seemed Her Hands Were Tied.
She Now Had To Marry Dominic.**

Her brother-in-law.

Her soon-to-be husband.

On the surface Dominic Roth was cool and arrogant toward her, but deep down there was a sexual fuse between them waiting to be lit. It had always been there, only she hadn't let herself think about it. She'd been a married woman and it wasn't something she'd wanted to acknowledge.

She still didn't want to acknowledge it. Call her naive but she wanted to believe that love and lust went hand in hand. With Dominic she knew it wouldn't. It would be lust, lust and more lust. There would be no love between them.

D0958059

Dear Reader,

Welcome to my exciting new Roth family series. This first story is about a marriage of convenience with a secret twist that I hope will tug at your heartstrings. It reminds me very much of the twists and turns in the glamorous soap operas I sometimes love to watch. Who's stealing from whom? Who's sleeping with whose husband? Whose child does she belong to? Who shot J.R.? ☺ I love the fact that in soap operas you can connect with all sorts of characters, both good and bad.

Yet when I read a romance I want my hero and heroine to be truly honorable, and if there are twists and turns I want their actions to be truly heroic. Dominic Roth is one such true hero. He could not refuse his dying brother's one last wish, in spite of all the problems he knew it would cause for himself. Cassandra Roth is a true heroine. She is hiding something, but she is doing it for the very best of reasons—to prevent her baby daughter being taken away from her. Dominic and Cassandra sacrifice everything in the name of love…and in the end love finds them both.

I hope you enjoy this book and the others that follow in this series.

Happy reading!

Maxine

MAXINE SULLIVAN

HIGH-SOCIETY SECRET BABY

Published by Silhouette Books
America's Publisher of Contemporary Romance

If you purchased this book without a cover you should be aware
that this book is stolen property. It was reported as "unsold and
destroyed" to the publisher, and neither the author nor the
publisher has received any payment for this "stripped book."

 **SILHOUETTE BOOKS**

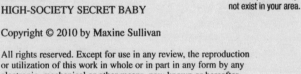

Recycling programs
for this product may
not exist in your area.

ISBN-13: 978-0-373-73034-6

HIGH-SOCIETY SECRET BABY

Copyright © 2010 by Maxine Sullivan

All rights reserved. Except for use in any review, the reproduction
or utilization of this work in whole or in part in any form by any
electronic, mechanical or other means, now known or hereafter
invented, including xerography, photocopying and recording, or in
any information storage or retrieval system, is forbidden without
the written permission of the editorial office, Silhouette Books,
233 Broadway, New York, NY 10279 U.S.A.

This is a work of fiction. Names, characters, places and incidents are
either the product of the author's imagination or are used fictitiously, and
any resemblance to actual persons, living or dead, business establishments,
events or locales is entirely coincidental.

This edition published by arrangement with Harlequin Books S.A.

For questions and comments about the quality of this book please contact us
at Customer_eCare@Harlequin.ca.

® and TM are trademarks of Harlequin Books S.A., used under license.
Trademarks indicated with ® are registered in the United States Patent
and Trademark Office, the Canadian Trade Marks Office and in other
countries.

Visit Silhouette Books at www.eHarlequin.com

Printed in U.S.A.

Books by Maxine Sullivan

Silhouette Desire

*The Millionaire's Seductive Revenge #1782
*The Tycoon's Blackmailed Mistress #1800
*The Executive's Vengeful Seduction #1818
Mistress & a Million Dollars #1855
The CEO Takes a Wife #1883
The C.O.O. Must Marry #1926
Valente's Baby #1949
His Ring, Her Baby #2008
High-Society Secret Baby #2021

*Australian Millionaires

MAXINE SULLIVAN

credits her mother for her lifelong love of romance novels, so it was a natural extension for Maxine to want to write her own romances. She thinks there's nothing better than being a writer and is thrilled to be one of the few Australians to write for the Silhouette Desire line.

Maxine lives in Melbourne, Australia, but over the years has traveled to New Zealand, the U.K. and the U.S.A. In her own backyard, her husband's job ensured they saw the diversity of the countryside, from the tropics to the Outback, country towns to the cities. She is married to Geoff, who has proven his hero status many times over the years. They have two handsome sons and an assortment of much-loved, previously abandoned animals.

Maxine would love to hear from you. She can be contacted through her Web site at www.maxinesullivan.com.

To my good friend Sandra Marton,
who is as wonderful as her books.

One

"Marry you?" Cassandra Roth whispered as she sank down on the leather sofa.

Dominic Roth stood in front of the terrace doors with the city of Melbourne's skyline in the distance behind him and watched his beautiful sister-in-law gasp in shock. He'd almost feel sorry for her if he didn't know her better. "That's right. You and I are getting married."

His voice seemed to draw her from herself, and she lifted her ash-blond head, her eyes clouding over. "But Liam's been dead only a week."

Pain clawed through him. "I know exactly how long my brother has been dead." And early December would never be the same for his family. The start of summer, then Christmas, would always hold the memory of Liam.

There was a flash of sympathy before she pulled back her slim shoulders. "And he was my husband."

"For less than three years. He was my brother for twenty-eight." Liam had been the youngest, Adam was two years older, and Dominic was two years older than Adam. Never had any of them dreamed that an illness would take Liam at such a young age.

"That's a low blow, Dominic," she admonished.

He kept any hint of remorse out of his expression. He wouldn't have said that to any other woman but this one. She'd married Liam only to get her hands on the Roth family fortune. His great-grandfather would roll over in his grave if he knew that Roth's, his Australian luxury goods department store chain, was keeping this woman in her own brand of luxury.

He reached inside the jacket of his business suit and pulled out an envelope. "I have a letter here. It's from Liam. He wanted me to give it to you. To explain."

Her finely arched eyebrows drew together. "Explain?"

"Why he wanted you to marry me."

Her blue eyes widened. "What! My husband *wanted* me to marry you?"

"He wanted his daughter to grow up a Roth."

Her forehead creased; her eyes looked confused. "But Nicole is already a Roth."

Something turned inside him. *He* knew that more than anyone.

"Liam wanted his daughter to *grow up* a Roth, living under the Roth name. He didn't want you marrying someone outside the family. He thought you might, especially considering your affair with Keith Samuels."

She drew in a sharp breath. "You know about that?"

"Liam told me."

"But—but it wasn't like that."

"No excuses please, Cassandra," he snapped, carrying the letter over to her. "I don't want to hear the details."

She stared up at him, a tremor touching her lips, but he

was unmoved by her performance. He thrust the sealed envelope at her and moved back to his original position, scrutinizing her as she tore open the envelope and began to read. How could any woman be so stunningly beautiful yet be so hard and demanding underneath? What was in the way she carried herself that was so deceptive? What was her allure for a man?

Her soft pink ensemble of matching trousers, camisole top and jacket projected an image of elegance and grace. Strappy sandals added style, as did the delicate gold earrings and thin gold chain at her neck. Her makeup was refined, her skin flawless, her ash-blond hair gently fluffed and falling down to her shoulders.

And that flawless face was white by the time she finished reading. "Did you read this?"

"No, but Liam apprised me of its contents when he gave it to me."

Something shifted in her expression, but it disappeared as she jumped to her feet, the letter held tightly in her hand. "I'm sorry, but I can't do this."

"I think you'll find you don't have a choice."

There was a fleeting pause. "Why do you say that?"

"The reading of Liam's will is tomorrow. I thought I'd break it to you beforehand to avoid a scene." Thank God his father had taken his mother away on the family yacht to mourn.

"A—a scene?"

"If you don't marry me within two weeks, the bulk of the estate will go to Nicole when she turns twenty-one, rather than being shared between you now. You'll receive only enough to live on, solely for Nicole's well-being, until then. If that happens, every cent you need will have to go through me."

"What!"

He would not let himself feel sorry for her. "Liam told me how much allowance you receive each month. He was extremely generous. I'd say you have a lot to lose, wouldn't you?"

Her throat convulsed. "But that was for—"

"There you have it," he said, cutting her off, not wanting to hear excuses.

"This is ridiculous! It's an abomination. I'll contest it."

"You could try. Liam tied it up pretty good. As it stands, you'll have just enough to live on, and certainly nothing like the standard of living you have now," he mocked, glancing around the room.

The spacious town house was a showcase of modern living, with a design reflecting space and light, a white-on-white decor, state-of-the-art technology second to none, and a private courtyard ideal for extensive entertaining. He'd been here only a few times, but he'd always thought it was ideal for them both.

Yet studying Cassandra now, he realized she didn't seem to fit in the place at all. Had it suited Liam more? And why suddenly *not* her? The coolness, the whiteness, the automation of it all *should* fit her, but it didn't, and he didn't know why it wasn't reflecting what he knew of this woman.

He grimaced to himself at that. Hell, what did he care, anyway? Damn Liam for entangling him in all this. If only he hadn't unknowingly gone to the hospital that day to see Liam during the artificial insemination process. If only...

"You forget that I have this town house, Dominic," she said, sounding more in control now. "I could sell it. Nicole and I could live on the proceeds."

Her voice drew him from his thoughts. "The town house

is in *my* name, Cassandra. Liam deeded it over to me a month ago."

She lost more color. "Oh, God, he didn't want me to get any of it, did he?"

"No, he didn't."

Hurt flashed across her face so fast, he almost missed it. He allowed her that. Having a husband do this to you wouldn't be an easy thing to accept, no matter that she'd done the wrong thing by Liam in the first place.

Of course, she'd never loved Liam. She'd proven that when she'd pushed him to go home to their parents' house to die, rather than letting him die in his own home with his wife beside him. As it should be. Oh, she'd acted like she'd been there for him until the end, and she'd cried after it was over, but a truly grieving widow? He didn't believe so.

"I'll say he wasn't in his right mind," she said, desperate now.

"His lawyer will attest to the opposite."

More panic flared in her eyes. "What's to stop me from marrying you, then getting the money and walking away?"

Dominic knew it was time to wrap this up. He didn't want to see this woman beg—not unless it was in the bedroom. At the thought, he could hear the blood fighting through his veins to get to her, like it always did.

It gave him the impetus to say what needed to be said. She was the mother of a nine-month-old Roth child—a child who was right now asleep in the bedroom and had no idea of what was going on out here in the living room with the adults. And whether either he or Cassandra liked it or not, this had to be done.

"If you don't marry me, or you marry me and then ask for a divorce, I'll fight for custody of Nicole."

She swayed a little and flopped back down on the sofa, closing her eyes. He went to go to her, then stopped. He had no doubt she loved her child now. It was her one and only saving grace, regardless that Liam had told him she hadn't wanted a baby at first. But he had to remember he was fighting for the *rights* of that child. Nicole deserved to be brought up a Roth.

If only he could put paid to all this by telling Cassandra the truth about her daughter. But dammit, he couldn't say a word. Not until the time was right. He'd promised Liam he'd keep the secret to himself until Nicole's future was cemented, and only after *he* and Cassandra were married. And then there were his parents to consider. He had to wait until their grief eased before he dumped another bombshell on them.

"Look around you," he said, letting his gaze sweep the magnificent living room. "You and Nicole are living a first-class lifestyle. You don't think a judge couldn't be persuaded that money and privilege aren't your child's right?"

All at once she had a fierce look about her. "A mother's love is more important."

"Yes, if you get a judge who believes love comes before the rest. Regardless of that, a wife who could be unfaithful to her husband would make the judge question that woman's morals, don't you think?"

"But I *wasn't* unfaithful," she said, turning pale.

"Save it for the judge, Cassandra."

She winced. He could see her balancing it all up. Then, "This is absurd," she burst out.

"I agree, but it's what Liam wanted, and as far as I'm concerned, I'm going to make sure my brother's dying wish is fulfilled."

His words hung in the air.

Then she shot him a penetrating look, bouncing back, like he knew she would. "Tell me, Dominic. What do you get out of all this if I marry you, besides a wife who doesn't love you or a child that isn't yours?"

His heart lurched. "I'll get the satisfaction of knowing my niece has a father."

"Why you? Why not Adam?"

Thoughts of her and Adam together were not pleasant. He loved his other brother, but Adam wasn't planning on getting married again, not after his wife died a few years ago in a car accident. Besides, *he* wasn't willing to share. It had been hard enough ignoring his lust for Cassandra as Liam's wife. He wouldn't go through that again. If marriage was the only option—and it was—then it would be with *him*.

"I'm the oldest. I'll do what's necessary."

Her cheeks took on some color, though whether through anger or embarrassment he couldn't tell. "There's something you've forgotten, Dominic. What about your parents?"

"They've lost a precious son, and now they'll have the chance to keep their grandchild in their lives. I think they'll understand, don't you?"

She blanched. "But they don't even like me."

"You did the wrong thing by their son. You expect they would?"

Her chin went up. "I married your brother for love, Dominic. Nothing else."

"Sure," he mocked.

She gave him one of her cool looks. "You've always thought I married him for his money, haven't you?"

"Not merely his money. There are a lot more things that go with being a Roth."

Her mouth took on a cynical twist. "Oh, I see. I was fostered, then adopted as a child, so automatically that makes me want what you have?" Her eyes held steady. "I thought you were more intelligent than that."

The comment stung. "My intelligence isn't at stake here."

"No, my future is, and that of my daughter's."

He hardened his heart. "It's only your daughter's future I'm concerned with."

"Thanks very much. Perhaps I should just hand her over and leave you to it?" she choked out.

Anger filled him. "You would do that?"

"Of course not!"

His heart settled, and then he recognized it was a real possibility. "How about a cool million for her?"

"Don't insult me, Dominic."

"Too low?"

She looked wounded but recovered. "This is my daughter, and I intend to keep her. Nicole comes first. She needs her mother. And *I* need her."

Relief filled him. He could handle knowing this woman was a gold digger and an adulterer, but the possibility of a child finding out her mother had given her away was something else.

"Then it's marriage or nothing," he stated firmly.

She looked down at the letter in her hand and swallowed. "I—"

"Yes or no, Cassandra?"

Seconds lapsed.

She took a ragged breath and lifted her head. "It looks like I don't have a choice."

"Neither do I, but this isn't about us."

"No, it's about my daughter, and she's the only reason I'll marry you, Dominic."

He smiled cynically. "Are you trying to dent my ego?"

"I haven't got a big enough jackhammer for that."

His lips twitched despite himself, and her mouth curved a hint and suddenly he was aware it wasn't the jackhammer he had to worry about. It was that wispy little smile he'd seen on those soft lips. Lips he intended to kiss one day soon.

"I'll make the arrangements," he said brusquely and strode from the house without another word. He had to remember that his younger brother had been sucker punched by this woman's beauty. Liam had given her the Roth name, a luxurious town house, furs, expensive jewelry, and she'd taken it all without a qualm.

Sure, she had come through for Liam and had proceeded with giving him the one thing he'd desperately wanted before he died—a child with whom to leave something of himself behind. But had it really been such a sacrifice? She would have known she was set for life by having a Roth child.

Of course, what she *didn't* know was that Liam's blood ties to his oldest brother had won out over conscience in the end. Blood ties through Nicole.

And one day Cassandra would have to know the truth. That the daughter she thought was her late husband's was actually *his*.

Cassandra stayed sitting long after her brother-in-law left, thankful Nicole was taking her afternoon nap.

The letter in her hand said it all.

Oh, God, how could Liam have done this to her? Liam, the man who'd totally swept her off her feet three years ago. A dashing young man who'd declared he'd fallen in love with her from the moment he'd seen her working behind the cosmetics counter at the Roth's flagship store in the city. He hadn't taken no for an answer. She wished he had.

Cassandra, forgive me for doing this, but I have no choice. I want Nicole to be raised a Roth.

Their marriage had been a sham almost from the start. She'd loved him, but Liam had wanted only a trophy wife and hadn't really loved her beyond her looks. He'd showered her with presents, but it had all been about putting her on display.

And then he'd accused her of having an affair with his friend Keith. He'd arrived at their house one day when she'd been home alone. She disliked Keith intensely, but she'd let him come in when he'd said he needed to talk to her. Once inside he'd followed her into the kitchen, where she'd gone to make coffee, and kissed her. Then Liam had come home unexpectedly and no amount of explaining that the kiss had been against her will had changed her husband's mind. Certainly Keith had played the innocent, even going so far as to say that she'd seduced him months ago and that he'd been trying to end their affair, no doubt covering himself in case his wife was ever to find out.

The day after all this, Liam's test results had come back with the worst kind of news and she hadn't the heart to leave him then. In sickness and in health... It had been their first anniversary.

It's not just for Nicole's sake. I want my parents to be involved in their granddaughter's life.

She hadn't been prepared for his next shock a few months later. Out of the blue he'd wanted to father a child so that a part of him would live on after he'd gone. Weakened from his condition's aggressive treatment, and no longer feeling attractive as a man, he'd then begged her to have his child by artificial insemination.

Nicole will be of great comfort to them in their grief. And that comforts me.

She'd said an adamant no at first, not wanting to bring a

child into the world for the wrong reasons. But he'd known she'd badly wanted a baby when they'd first married, and he'd assured her their child would be well looked after by his family if anything ever happened to *her*.

Still she'd hesitated.

And in the midst of this her beloved adoptive father had needed full-time care after a stroke, and there was no way her adoptive sister could help financially. Liam—always one to grasp an opportunity—had dangled another carrot in front of her by promising to place Joe in an expensive nursing home and pay all costs if she had his baby.

She'd finally agreed.

I want you to marry Dominic. It's the only way I can be sure Nicole stays a Roth. He will take care of her.

At Liam's suggestion, the half-million-dollar-bond for the nursing home had been placed in her account, and Liam's accountant had been putting a certain amount into her bank account each month, along with her monthly allowance. She'd been happy with that. It suited her to keep an eye on things herself.

Today she'd discovered that all money had been stopped. Now she knew why, God rest Liam's soul. Had he planned this all along? Or was this something that had occurred to him near the end? She'd probably never know the answer.

If you refuse, then I've left a letter with my lawyer to give to Dominic. It contains the truth.

She'd never wanted to get involved with another Roth again, but it seemed her hands were tied. She now had to marry Dominic.

Her brother-in-law.

Her soon-to-be husband.

On the surface Dominic Roth was cool and arrogant toward her, but deep down there was a sexual fuse between them waiting to be lit. It had always been there, only she hadn't let herself think about it previously. She'd been a married woman, and it wasn't something she'd wanted to acknowledge. Despite Liam's accusations, she would never be unfaithful to her husband. Not with his brother and not with Keith.

She still didn't want to acknowledge any sexual desire for a man she disliked. Call her naive, but she wanted to believe that love and lust went hand in hand. With Dominic she knew they wouldn't. It would be lust, lust and more lust. There would be no love between them.

I forgive you for your affair with Keith; I blame myself for that. And I forgive you for forcing me to pay you to have my baby, darling. I know you didn't want a child at first and that you did it for me, despite taking the money. And I know the truth, if it all comes out, will hurt you.

She swallowed hard as she looked down at the letter and let the words sink in. The truth? There was no truth in his words, not about the affair and not about Nicole. How could Liam lie like that? He was virtually saying she was an adulterer who'd "sold" her body to have the baby of a dying man. It hadn't been like that at all. She had wanted a baby, but had hesitated for various reasons. Saying yes hadn't been about the money. It had not been for herself.

Marry Dominic and raise Nicole together as a family. He'll be a wonderful father. And she's a beautiful little girl who deserves to be loved for herself.

If you refuse, Dominic already has my full blessing to fight for custody of Nicole. The letter with my lawyer detailing everything will be used against you in court.

The threat sent chills down her spine. Dominic could easily have the family lawyers paint her in a bad light for custody of Nicole. They'd have no hesitation in twisting things, especially if they dragged Keith into court. She was certain he would perjure himself to protect his marriage.

And after proving her a liar, the lawyers would simply have to point out that her monthly allowance had been increased at the same time her father had been put in the nursing home, not to mention that the five hundred thousand dollars for the bond had been given to her at the same time she'd been artificially inseminated. They'd only have to search her records, going back a few years, to discover that. And then it would "prove" she'd blackmailed her husband.

The letter will be destroyed six months after you marry Dominic. Look on this as my legacy to you all.

She could fight Dominic, of course, but what chance would an adopted kid from a low-income family have at winning against a wealthy, upstanding family like the Roths? Her parents-in-law would dislike her even more once they learned the so-called "truth." They would want revenge, too.

So marry Dominic she would.

And let him think the worst of her she would.

She didn't want him to know anything he could use in court against her. An unfaithful wife "paid" to have a baby wasn't something an unsympathetic judge could choose to look kindly on, no matter the circumstances or what good she'd done with the money.

She wouldn't risk being labeled an unfit wife and mother.

She would risk nothing where her daughter was concerned.

Two

The wedding ceremony was held in the plush surroundings of Dominic's office in the city a few days later, in what had to be one of the quickest services on record. Even the hasty ceremony for her and Liam had been longer than this.

She wouldn't have wanted it any other way. Dominic had juggled his schedule to fit this in, and it somehow seemed appropriate. This wasn't a love match between them. His fleeting kiss on the side of her mouth sealing their marriage a few minutes ago was testament to that.

Fleeting but potent.

"I'm glad you dressed appropriately for your wedding," he murmured sardonically as his personal assistant, Janice, hurried the marriage celebrant out the door.

Cassandra casually patted the jeweled hair stick in her French twist. She thought the short satin dress with the chic bolero jacket was a nice touch, especially in black. "I'm a widow, remember?"

"Not any longer."

She winced inwardly, but wouldn't let him know it. "Next time I marry, I'll wear gray then."

His brows flattened. "There won't be a next time," he all but snapped.

She held his gaze, then looked away to where the other witness to their marriage—his brother Adam—was opening a bottle of champagne. Oh, God, she didn't feel in the least like celebrating being married again. There was absolutely nothing to celebrate in this travesty of a ceremony. It was the reason she hadn't brought Nicole today or told her sister, and Dominic hadn't pressed her about it, either.

Thankfully his parents were still away on their yacht, mourning in seclusion and sparing her their presence today. Everyone had been sworn to secrecy to protect them until their return. Despite their feelings about her—and, dear God, that had been Liam's doing—she didn't dislike her parents-in-law. The opposite, in fact.

"Incidentally," Dominic suddenly rasped in her ear, "you look very beautiful in black."

A touch of heat rose up her neck as she watched him walk away in a dark business suit that made him look both powerful and sexy. That was the first time he'd ever made a personal comment to her, and it was devastating to know her senses were leaping all over the place. She wished she could deny it, but there had always been this "hint" of something more between them, always possibilities that could never be realized.

Until today.

Just then, the champagne cork popped.

"Here we go, Cassandra," Janice said, coming toward her. "A glass of champagne for the bride."

Cassandra mustered a smile. "Thank you."

Janice swung around to encompass the men. "Now that

we all have some champagne, I'd like to make a toast." She held her glass in the air. "To Cassandra and Dominic."

There was a moment's hesitation by everyone.

Then Adam raised his glass. "To Cassandra and Dominic," he said, his face as enigmatic as his brother's.

Cassandra inclined her head at her brother-in-law. Adam was too young to be a widower, and Cassandra suspected that was why he spent so much time traveling around Australia, going from store to store to make sure things were running smoothly, checking their suppliers to make sure the quality of their luxury goods remained exceptional. She hadn't really got to know him well, and his wife's death had happened before she'd married Liam, but he was another one who'd always been slightly aloof with her, though there had never been the sexual awareness between them like there was between her and Dominic.

Yet Adam was like Dominic in many respects. Handsome. Confident. Mature. And with the sex appeal that the Roth sons had brought into the world at the expense of other men.

"Thank you both," Dominic said, drawing Cassandra from her thoughts. He looked at her and held up his glass. "To us," he toasted, a challenge in his eyes.

She had the image of him holding up a starting pistol. *Let the games begin.*

"To us," she replied, giving him a cool look that said she would be ready for whatever he threw at her.

As if he'd read her thoughts, his eyes narrowed.

"Cassandra, I guess you'll have to change your address now," Janice observed, then looked at her boss. "Or perhaps *you're* going to move in with Cassandra and Nicole?"

"No. Cassandra and Nicole will be moving in with me." Dominic's clipped tones brooked no discussion.

Two spots of red appeared in Janice's cheeks, and

Cassandra felt sorry for her, but the other woman should be used to her boss by now.

And Cassandra had to admit she was glad about moving out of the town house she'd shared with Liam. Of course moving *in* with Dominic wasn't what she wanted, either.

"At least you don't have to change your surname," Adam joked, and Cassandra smiled to ease the tension in the room.

"I hadn't thought of that, Adam," she said.

Dominic put his glass down on the desk. "We'd better get going," he stated coldly, and Cassandra had the feeling he wasn't pleased about her smiling at his brother. Did he think she would seduce Adam?

Probably.

He had no need to be concerned about her with Adam, she mused, more concerned at the thought of leaving with Dominic right now and starting their future together.

She didn't have time to think further. Before she knew it, he had said his goodbyes and was leading her from the room and along the carpeted corridor. She tingled at his touch.

Once in the private elevator, she moved out of reach. "It was hardly worth the trouble of dressing up," she said to cover her reaction.

His gaze raked boldly over her black dress, from breast to midthigh hem, his look both appreciative and condemning. "You're lucky I didn't see what you were wearing beforehand."

Her heart bumped her ribs. "Why?"

"Let's say I would have waited while you changed."

She squared her shoulders. "And if I refused?"

"The ceremony would have been delayed."

She opened her mouth.

"Let it go, Cassandra. It's done now. You look beautiful

no matter what color you're dressed in." A new glint entered his eyes. "And no matter what you wear."

She was grateful that the elevator stopped then. His BMW and a driver were waiting as they stepped out into the underground car park. Soon they were whizzing out of the city, toward his home at Sandringham, a bayside suburb southeast of Melbourne, renowned for its yacht club and golf course.

"We've got a bit of a drive ahead of us," he said beside her on the backseat just as her heartbeat had slowed.

"We do?" *Oh, no.* "Please tell me we're not going on a honeymoon, Dominic?" The family had a holiday home in tropical Queensland.

Something flickered at the back of his eyes. "Not exactly. A friend has lent us his bush retreat not far from Lorne on the Great Ocean Road. We're going there for a week."

A week with Dominic in a secluded cottage? It was going to be bad enough settling into married life with this man...*sharing a bed with this man*...but she hadn't expected they'd have too much time alone together. He had a busy life. And she intended to keep busy, too, wanting something more than being a trophy wife, like she'd been to Liam.

At the thought of being considered nothing *but* a trophy wife, Cassandra knew she had to stand up for herself—and keep on standing up for herself—until Dominic realized she wouldn't be pushed around.

"You really should have told me about all this," she said, sending him an irritated look.

He turned his head toward her. "Why? What good would it have done?"

"I might have had my own plans."

"Then you would have had to change them."

Oh, he was so smug.

"Like I'd change my dress? Don't be too sure, Dominic," she said coolly, then looked out her side window, intentionally dismissive.

Tension strung between them.

Then his cell phone rang, and he reached into his pocket and answered it. He was still talking on the phone when they turned onto a tree-lined street close to the beach. At the end, behind a pair of high gates that were now automatically opening, they drove through the grounds to a mansion nestled in sun-soaked seclusion.

It was a glorious house, but Cassandra had been in no mood to appreciate it earlier, when his driver had collected her and they'd dropped Nicole off here. And she was in no mood to appreciate it now as the driver halted behind a luxury SUV parked in front of the steps.

As soon as they were out of the car, Dominic dismissed the driver, who then drove off in the BMW just as the housekeeper opened the door, carrying Nicole.

"Congratulations, Mrs. Roth," Nesta said, coming toward them.

Cassandra's smile was genuine as she lifted Nicole from her. There had been a kindness in the other woman's eyes earlier that had made her think they could be on friendly terms. "Thank you, Nesta. Has she been a good girl?"

"Oh, yes. She's a darling little thing, and I'd be happy to babysit her anytime." Nesta touched Nicole's cheek. "I bet she takes after her mother."

Cassandra laughed. "Only when it comes to luxuriously long baths." Nicole loved playing in the water at bath time, and *she* loved to lie back in the bubbles and soak when she had the chance. When she was growing up, there had never been the opportunity to take too long in the bathroom.

As if she agreed with her mother, Nicole babbled something, making them chuckle. She could always rely on her beautiful daughter to make her smile, Cassandra mused, stroking her daughter's blond curls away from her chubby face.

All at once, she caught Dominic's eye. He was staring back at her, a muscle pulsing in his cheek, his eyes dangerously dark and drawing her into that web of physical awareness between them again. Her throat went dry.

The moment was broken by Nesta. "I'd better let you get on your way," the middle-aged woman said, oblivious to the undercurrents. "Everything's ready and in the car, Mr. Roth."

There was a small pause; then Dominic's expression became inscrutable again. "Thanks, Nesta," he said, but he was still looking at Cassandra. "Do you want to change your clothes before we leave?"

She noticed he had taken off his jacket and tie and was looking tantalizingly informal. "No. I'll wait." She wasn't ready to go inside to the bedroom she'd share with him on their return. Right now it seemed too intimate.

His mouth compressed. "It'll be hours before we get there," he pointed out.

"That's okay."

His eyes turned cool. "Suit yourself." He strode toward the SUV.

His coldness was discouraging, but there was nothing for it except to follow him, but before she could move, Nesta put a hand on her arm.

"Don't let him leave yet, Mrs. Roth. I'll just be a jiffy." The housekeeper hesitated, and thinking the woman had forgotten something, Cassandra nodded that she would wait.

Nesta hurried inside, and Cassandra went to put Nicole in the vehicle. She was mildly surprised Dominic wasn't using the Porsche she'd seen occasionally at his parents' place, but this was more a family vehicle and perfect for long trips and children. It looked brand-new and probably was, but at least he'd thought to have an infant's car seat included.

Evidently that was as far as his thoughtfulness went, she decided as he stood at the open driver's door, watching her strap Nicole in the rear seat. By the time she'd straightened, Nesta had returned.

"Here we go, Mrs. Roth." The housekeeper handed her a black cashmere cardigan. "You can take off the jacket and put this on. It'll be more comfortable for you."

Cassandra was touched by the woman's thoughtfulness. "Thank you, Nesta." She slid out of the bolero jacket and replaced it with the refined knitwear. The material was light enough not to be too hot to wear on an early summer's day like today, and it immediately downgraded her wedding outfit to a more stylishly casual look.

"There. That's more comfortable for you," Nesta said, beaming at her.

"One more thing." To complete the look, Cassandra removed the jeweled hair stick and released her French twist, letting her hair tumble to her shoulders. "That's better."

"You're so beautiful, Mrs. Roth."

Cassandra smiled. "I don't know about that, Nesta."

Suddenly Dominic muttered something under his breath and seated himself behind the steering wheel. "Come on. We'd better be on our way."

Cassandra winked at Nesta, but underneath she was beginning to fume. Once they were off down the driveway, she was tempted to say something about his attitude toward his housekeeper, but his hard profile made her hold the words back.

She would pick her battles.

Nonetheless, as she glanced behind to check on Nicole, a slither of apprehension appeared as she remembered him watching her strap her daughter into the infant seat. He'd been remote then, too. Would he continue to ignore his new stepdaughter? Would he merely supply the material things but not offer Nicole more than that?

Of course, she had to admit he had only ever seen his niece a handful of times since her birth. And some men were quite indifferent to children, especially when they were small. Then perhaps she was getting ahead of herself, she decided, taking a calming breath. She couldn't imagine that a man so concerned for his niece's well-being would be so heartless as to ignore the child entirely.

Feeling better, she breathed easier now, and they drove south for a while without talking. Periodically she checked on Nicole in the back, happy to see her little girl playing with one of her stuffed animals.

The next time she looked, Nicole's eyes were shut. "She's asleep," she murmured, more to herself than anything, her heart melting with motherly love.

"That was fast." He sounded bemused.

She felt more cordial toward him now. "You obviously don't know children," she said lightly.

He gave a wry smile. "No doubt I'll learn."

Her heart bounced. His comment said he fully intended to get to know Nicole. Thank God!

Quickly she turned to the front and rested her head back against her own seat, not wanting him to know she was such a marshmallow over her child.

"Take a nap if you want."

She glanced sideways at him. "No, I'm fine."

"You look exhausted to me."

Her lips twisted. "Gee, thanks."

There was no smile on his lips now. "This break will do you and Nicole good."

Something more tender stirred inside her. "Thank you." She wouldn't let herself linger on that, though. "But please don't let me stop you from coming back to the city and working. I can look after myself and Nicole for the week."

His jaw set, and they seemed to be back to square one. "Adam can run the place without me for a week." He paused, then admitted, "I could do with a break myself."

The admission took her by surprise, and in spite of herself, compassion inched its way through her. He might try to look like he didn't feel things too deeply, but she suspected he did. His younger brother's death would have been a tremendous loss to him.

"Have you heard from your parents?" she asked for something to say, her heart going out to Laura and Michael.

"No, and I don't expect to. I want them to forget all about us while they're on the *Lady Laura*."

"I'm glad they took the time for themselves," she said softly, receiving a sharp look from him in return. She sighed to herself. Did he have to believe she was incapable of feeling compassion?

After that they drove without talking. Nicole woke up cranky just as they were driving onto the ferry at Sorrento, but a diaper change and a bottle of formula soon had her returning to her sweet self.

Then they went up on deck and enjoyed the sunshine and brilliant views of Port Phillip Bay as they journeyed across to Queenscliff, but it was the dolphins swimming alongside the ferry that was the highlight of the forty-minute trip.

Cassandra felt refreshed by the time they were driving

again, and she could see that Dominic was looking less strained around the eyes, as well.

Eventually they joined the Great Ocean Road, a magnificent marvel of a road built with picks and shovels by returning servicemen of the First World War in honor of their fallen comrades. It was a stunning drive, challenging and exhilarating, with rugged coastline on one side of the road and the natural bush on the other.

When they came around another bend and more spectacular sights greeted them, Cassandra couldn't help but exclaim anew every time.

"I can't believe you haven't been down this way before," Dominic said, giving her a curious look before concentrating on the windy road ahead.

"I wish I had. It's breathtaking." And that was all she said. She still wasn't sure what Dominic knew about her childhood, but he must not know about her father being in the nursing home or he would have said something. If Dominic suspected anything amiss, she would know about it.

And they were married now, she told herself, so surely she could relax a little. She'd done what he'd wanted. Only if she decided to leave him might he discover the money Liam had paid her.

It was around seven that evening when they drove through Lorne, a seaside resort town set between the sparkling waters off its beautiful beach and the lush forests of the Otway Ranges. It was a lovely town dressed up with Christmas decorations, reminding her that Christmas was only a few weeks away. She didn't feel like celebrating the festive season, but she would make the effort for Nicole's sake.

"We'll take a look around tomorrow," Dominic said,

slowing down and peering out his side window at the street signs.

"What are you looking for?"

"I can't remember which road I'm supposed to take."

"Why not stop and ask someone?"

"No need."

She pointed to the small café and suggested, "Pull over there and check with someone in one of the shops."

He shook his head absentmindedly. "No, I'll find it." He continued to drive, and she gave a small snort. He glanced at her. "What's that for?"

"You're a typical male. You'd rather chance getting lost than ask for directions."

His eyes were amused. "Why ask someone when I can find it myself?" He looked back at the road, then put on his indicator to turn right. "Like now."

She blinked. "How do you know this is the right one?"

"I just do."

She smiled and rolled her eyes, but decided not to say anything more until they reached their destination.

Or not.

It was quite a few miles before they turned into a meandering dirt driveway. And there, hidden behind towering gum trees, was the two-story cottage in a tranquil bush oasis. He'd found it like he had some sort of mental tracking device.

"Pure luck," she quipped.

Okay, so she'd been wrong back there. This man wasn't typical at all. Not only would he always find his way in the world, but he would do it *his* way.

He chuckled and she laughed and a rare moment of ease slipped between them as he parked. They got out of the vehicle, and she unbuckled Nicole from her seat while Dominic removed some of the luggage.

"There's a woman who comes every second day," he said as they made their way up the wooden steps. "She'll tidy up and make sure we're stocked up on food."

Cassandra hadn't needed to do housework since before her marriage to Liam, but that wasn't the case growing up. Her parents had believed everyone did their fair share, and she'd had no problem with that.

She adjusted Nicole on her hip. "I'm sure I can manage to cook and clean for the week."

"No. You're to rest," he said, spurting warmth through her. It had been a while since a man had been concerned for her welfare.

He opened the front door, putting the suitcases down inside before keying in some numbers on a high-tech security pad. The place was evidently alarmed to the hilt, and Cassandra supposed that made sense, seeing there were no other houses close by.

It was a delightful "cottage" and bigger than it looked, with a welcome sense of space. The rustic living room had cathedral ceilings, and the country kitchen was outfitted with the latest appliances. There was even a fully equipped study-cum-office. A deck at the back led down to a swimming pool with a forest backdrop.

A set of stairs at either end of the house led up to the bedrooms, and as they climbed one set, she tried not to think too hard about the coming night. The first couple of rooms were sizable and charming. The third one held a double bed and shared a bathroom with the next room, as well as even having a small refrigerator with tea and coffee facilities in one corner. A child's crib had been placed on one side of the room.

Dominic put the suitcases down beside the bed. "I

...ld hide behind nothing...until she could hide *nothing* ...m him.

And then he'd gone and changed his mind. Of course, ...knew why. Watching her taking care of Nicole on the ...ive down here had gotten to him and had made her seem ...ore loving and less the gold digger, more sensitive.

And now there she was, unaware in her sleep that she ...ad shown him it wasn't an act. That shielding his— *...heir*—daughter from falling off the bed was as natural as ...reathing.

He ran a hand through his hair. Damn Liam for asking him to take on such a huge responsibility. And damn himself for giving in to a dying man. God in heaven, agreeing to substitute his sperm for the artificial insemination process had all sounded so...bearable at the time, yet that hadn't been the case. From the moment he'd agreed to Liam's request, nothing had been the same.

"Do this one last thing for me," Liam had hurriedly pleaded when Dominic had walked into the hospital room and found his brother alone. Liam was crying, distraught because he'd convinced Cassandra to have his baby, but he no longer wanted to chance that baby inheriting his disease, and nothing Dominic said would ease his mind. The disease wasn't genetic, but Liam had recently been given a new and more powerful drug to help hold the disease at bay, and he was concerned it might have harmed his sperm. It had broken Dominic's heart to see his beloved brother reduced to this. Without further thought, he had taken the sterilized jar and stridden into the bathroom, where he'd done what he had to do.

How could he not?

Afterward he'd been full of self-recrimination as he'd wondered where it all would lead. His brother was

thought you might like to share this room with Nicole," he said, gob-smacking her. He paused. "It makes sense for you to sleep with her."

Cassandra couldn't help it. She stared at him. She'd never expected this. All at once she wondered if he didn't want to make love to her, then rejected the idea. She could feel his desire every time he looked her way.

"I'll leave you to change into something more comfortable. Nesta packed what she thought would be necessary." His eyes rested on her, sliding down over her black dress, the top of which was covered by the black cashmere cardigan. "No more black, okay?"

She cleared her throat and tried to switch gears in her mind. "Er...I like black."

"You weren't wearing black the other day."

She realized he was talking about when he'd dropped by the other day with the letter from Liam. "I was at home then, that's why."

"No more, Cassandra. Nicole should have her mother dressed in bright clothes, not dark."

He had her there.

She nodded. "You're right."

He left with a satisfied look in his eyes, but she didn't mind. He was, after all, thinking of Nicole.

He shut the door behind him, and she let out a sigh of relief. She had no idea why he was allowing her time to get used to him, but she was very grateful for it. Who'd have thought he'd be so caring?

There wasn't time for further introspection. She changed out of her wedding dress and cardigan and into slacks and a knit top, then took Nicole down to the kitchen for dinner. She could hear Dominic talking on the telephone in the bedroom across the hallway. No doubt it was about business.

Her daughter was usually a good eater, but after only a few mouthfuls Nicole decided she didn't want to eat tonight. She clamped her bow-shaped mouth shut, the look in her dark eyes reminding Cassandra of Liam, as if she were trying to gauge how far to push. Of course, that was more a Roth trait than not, Cassandra admitted, thinking of Dominic, as well.

"Come on, sweetie," she coaxed. "You need to eat."

Nicole didn't budge. She started to get whiny, becoming really out of sorts now.

"Need a hand with anything?"

Cassandra looked up to see Dominic stepping into the kitchen. She groaned inwardly. An upset demeanor wouldn't exactly endear Nicole to her new stepfather. Then she winced at her thoughts. A child wasn't for show only. Dominic would need to learn to accept these moments.

"Thanks, anyway," she said, wiping Nicole's hands with some paper towel. "But it's past her bedtime, so I might just put her straight to bed with a bottle. She'll feel better once she's had a good night's sleep." *She* was starting to feel the effort of the day herself now.

He leaned up against the counter and watched her. "Don't put her to bed on my account."

"I won't." She appreciated the comment as she lifted Nicole out of the high chair. "If you don't mind, I'll stay with her until she settles."

He stared at her a heartbeat longer than necessary, and she didn't understand why. Then she realized he was looking at both her and Nicole, as if coming to terms with having a family now. She felt sorry for him right then. It was a big adjustment to make.

"I don't mind," he finally said, not giving anything away. "We'll have dinner when you come back."

She nodded, then grabbed a bottle of formula from the

refrigerator and carried Nicole from the room. co
wanted her bottle, Cassandra would heat it ups fro
than hang around down here any longer.

As for herself, she wasn't sure she could ea he
despite the appetizing plates of seafood she'd se d
refrigerator. Dominic was being generous in allo m
time to get used to him, but the specter of eventuall
to share his bed was still in the background. h

When Cassandra didn't come back within thirty m
Dominic went looking for her. Her bedroom door wa
and all was quiet, so he carefully opened it.

And found them both asleep.

The sight drew him across the room to stand look
down at them. The double bed had been pushed up agai
one wall, and Cassandra had placed Nicole next to her, ha
curling around the infant to stop her from wiggling onto th
floor. It was clear the two had been facing each other and
probably playing before dropping off to sleep, and even in
sleep a mother's protective hand rested on her daughter's
diapered bottom.

Something clutched inside his chest and tightened. Trying to ignore it, he pulled up the spare blanket at the end of the bed. He doubted they'd wake before morning.

After covering them up, he left the room and went to pour himself a measure of rum, the picture of Cassandra's long legs and the curve of her hip encased in slacks accompanying him out to the deck.

What on earth was he thinking by not taking her to his bed? He certainly hadn't planned it that way, not after the years of wanting this woman. Her cool poise was a turn-on, and he'd fully intended to have her in his bed at the first opportunity, heating her up and melting her down until she dying, and the mother of *his* child was a woman he didn't respect.

Later he'd had to watch Cassandra grow beautifully big with *his* child, and he'd stayed away as much as possible, unable to bear it. But the satisfaction in Liam's eyes had told him he'd done the right thing, no matter what. Liam had been so happy for his wife, who had bloomed throughout her pregnancy.

Then after the birth, Liam had called him to the hospital to see the new baby. And it had taken only one look at his daughter for Dominic to fall in love. She was a part of him. He would die for this child.

Three

Cassandra woke six hours later!

Nicole slept on, and that meant it was a good opportunity to take a shower. But first, Cassandra checked the cell phone she kept on vibration in her purse, making sure there had been no calls from the nursing home about her father. She didn't dare call them, either, or they might ask about the money. She would sort it out next week, when she returned to Melbourne.

The noise of the shower must have woken her daughter, because Nicole was awake and babbling to herself when Cassandra came out of the bathroom. *Too precious,* she mused as she went about changing her daughter's diaper before getting dressed herself in another pair of casual slacks and a knit top to hold off a slight morning chill. Then they headed to the kitchen for breakfast.

Dominic was sitting at the table, reading the newspaper and drinking coffee. He looked up, and at the speed of light his eyes swept over her, his gleam of approval warming her for an instant. She wasn't used to his open admiration, and for a split second she had to catch her breath, not the least because he looked so handsome in a steel-blue polo shirt that stretched across his broad chest.

Then she forced her legs to move. "I'm sorry about missing dinner last night," she said, carrying Nicole over to the high chair beside the table. "I fell asleep."

He folded the paper and put it to the side. "That's okay. I had an early night myself."

She could feel herself blushing. Would they ever be having early nights *together?* She kept her eyes averted while she secured Nicole, then went to prepare her daughter's breakfast, not allowing herself to think beyond the moment. It was best this way.

All was quiet as she mixed the baby cereal. Curious, she stole a glance over her shoulder and saw Dominic sitting there, looking at Nicole with a tender expression on his face. Her heart did a flip. Clearly he wasn't as unemotional about his brother's child as she'd suspected.

By the time she came back to the table, the tender look had disappeared and he was leaning back in his chair, drinking coffee.

"I thought we might go into Lorne after breakfast," he said as she sat down opposite him. "We can take a look around the town. There's plenty of stores if you need anything. Or we could walk along the beach."

"That would be nice." She placed a spoonful of cereal in Nicole's mouth. The little girl swallowed it quickly. Heavens, the poor kid was hungry, and was it any wonder? It had been over six hours since she'd had that bottle in the middle of the night, and before that she'd barely eaten anything at dinner.

All at once, Cassandra's own stomach cramped with hunger. She'd hardly eaten a thing yesterday.

"She likes her food," Dominic noted.

Cassandra smiled as she fed Nicole another spoonful of the mush, narrowly missing. "Yes, she does."

"It can be pretty messy feeding an infant, can't it?" Dominic said, and she looked up to see him watching her.

"She's just getting her coordination skills."

"You don't mind being splashed with her breakfast?"

She laughed. "Not when my daughter is the one doing it."

It was meant as a lighthearted comment, but all at once the moment went beyond Nicole.

Suddenly it was about *her* and Dominic and his reaction to her smile.

She watched as his gaze dropped to her mouth...watched as deep down she knew that he wanted to kiss her.... Then slowly...slowly...his eyes inched upward again.

And locked on hers.

She could feel herself being drawn into them.

"Um...speaking of food, I think I'll make myself some toast." Jumping to her feet, she took the cereal bowl over to the sink and rinsed it.

A lengthy pause went on behind her, but she ignored it until Dominic's chair scraped the floor as he stood up. "I've got some calls to make." He strode to the doorway. "Let me know when you're ready to go. No hurry."

It was crazy that her hands were shaking as she dropped the bread in the toaster. It was equally as crazy that this "thing" between her and Dominic was gathering strength. It was like all bets were off now that they were married.

Or perhaps she just needed food in her stomach,

she joked, trying to keep things inside herself on an even keel.

An hour later, after she had given Nicole a quick bath, had dressed her in some cute little overalls, and had changed her own top from the cereal-stained one, she went looking for Dominic. She found him on the deck, talking on his cell phone, but he wrapped up the conversation and they were soon on their way.

The ride into Lorne was quite pleasant, and soon they were strolling along the main street, past stylish shops and cosmopolitan restaurants in a beachside atmosphere. Dominic had offered to push Nicole's stroller, and Cassandra secretly watched him and couldn't help but think he actually looked a tad proud to be pushing her daughter around like this.

What wasn't to be proud of? Cassandra mused to herself, being the proud mama herself.

"What are you smiling at?" he asked, catching her unawares. She hadn't realized she'd been so obvious.

She went to tell him, then thought better of it. She didn't want him becoming self-conscious in the way he treated her daughter. Then she smiled to herself. *Dominic self-conscious? That'll be the day!*

"Who wouldn't feel like smiling in such a beautiful town?" she replied.

He shot her a dry look.

After that they spent another hour walking around. Then Dominic insisted they have lunch in one of the more upmarket restaurants, but it was such a warm day that Cassandra suggested an outdoor café overlooking the sheltered bay. He looked at her oddly, but soon she was feeding Nicole her lunch from a jar of baby food, and then they ate fish and chips that tasted divine because she hadn't eaten or done something like this in years. Cassandra could feel herself unwinding, and even Dominic looked more relaxed again.

They decided to go back to the house after that, where she put Nicole down for her afternoon nap, then grabbed a book from the living room while Dominic went off to work in the study.

Glad to have some time alone, Cassandra donned sunglasses and took her book outside, kicked off her sandals and stretched out on the lounger by the pool. The sun had grown hotter, and as she focused on the sound of cicadas in the surrounding bushland, the tension sapped from her.

She was deep in the story when Dominic sat down on the lounger near her, having swapped his trousers for casual cargo pants, his blue polo shirt hugging his chest, a thick paperback in one hand, dark glasses hiding his eyes.

Startled, she said the first thing that came to mind. "I didn't know you liked to read."

"Well, there you go," he mocked. "You learn something new every day." And they were back to being adversaries again.

Stupidly disappointed, she quickly looked down at the title of his book. "You read science fiction obviously."

He indicated her book with a derisive twist of his lips. "And you read romance."

Thankfully her sunglasses covered her eyes. "Why not?" she said as casually as she could, not wanting him to see his comment upset her. She wouldn't give him that power over her.

"It's not exactly your...forte, is it?"

He was just trying to goad her. "So you don't believe in true love, Dominic?" she challenged.

"What I believe doesn't matter."

"That's not the impression I get." This was about him

believing her unfaithful, so it *did* matter. It affected how he was treating her. In his eyes, she was only after the good life and nothing more. He thought her a woman totally incapable of loving a man for himself alone.

Suddenly sick at heart, she closed her book and got to her feet. "I think I hear Nicole waking up." She started to walk off, aware of his eyes following her.

"Cassandra?"

She took a few more steps, then stopped to look at him.

"Bring Nicole for a dip in the pool."

Her upset heart tilted inside her chest. She'd been putting off the moment when *she* had to wear her bikini in front of Dominic.

"Or are you scared of the water?" he drawled.

She had the feeling he'd guessed why she hesitated. "I love the water," she said, keeping her voice even despite her increasingly racing heart.

A second lapsed as he stilled—and the air thickened with sensuality. "Oh, that's right. You like to take very long and luxurious baths, don't you?"

The sun instantly felt hotter.

She moistened her dry lips. "We'll be back in a little while," she said, spinning away, heart thumping, knowing that the scrap of bikini Nesta had packed for her wasn't something she'd normally wear. Even before she'd given birth to Nicole, the bikini would have been on the smallish side, but these days her breasts were slightly fuller, her hips a touch curvier.

Darn, she should have bought herself a new bikini in town this morning. It would have been the perfect opportunity to buy something a little less revealing, but just being in Dominic's presence all morning had put a stop to rational thought.

Perhaps she could pretend it had been forgotten to be packed, after all. She pulled a face. Needless to say she could envision his reply to that.

Wear nothing.

Dominic almost expected to see his sunglasses steam up as he watched Cassandra walk away with a slight sway to her hips. He shouldn't be thinking about her in either a luxurious bath or a bikini. He didn't need any more of a vivid imagination right now, not when he was trying to ignore the picture of him running his hands down her slender back and over the gentle swell of those feminine hips. He was a man who couldn't take much more of this.

Of her.

Dammit, how did she do it? How did she manage to take a highly controlled man like himself and nearly send him over the edge with wanting her? How did she shoot need through every part of him as if she had the combination to his desire? And more importantly, why was he letting her get away with it?

Pushing to his feet, he stripped down to his swimming briefs and was in the water by the time she returned, walking toward him in a Pacific-blue bikini that tore his imagination to shreds.

Was she deliberately teasing him? Or was Nesta? He'd told his housekeeper to make sure Cassandra had a swimsuit to wear this weekend, but he hadn't expected these little triangles of cloth that left a *whole* lot of skin bare. God, he couldn't deny Cassandra had the body of a goddess and the perfect figure to wear such a skimpy thing. He couldn't even tell that she'd had a baby nine months ago.

And then he saw her begin to blush. It started in her

cheeks then spread downward over all that bare skin, and no doubt under the material, as well. Yet who would expect her to be so easily embarrassed? She was an enigma.

She cleared her throat. "Er…could you take Nicole for a moment?"

He heard the words, and he forced his focus to shift away from the bathing beauty…to the little beauty she carried. Cassandra had crouched down near the edge of the pool and was holding her daughter toward him.

His daughter.

All at once it hit him. He swallowed hard. So far he'd managed not to actually hold Nicole in his arms, fearful of giving himself away to Cassandra too soon.

"Dominic?"

He moved forward in the water and held out his arms.

And Nicole reached out to him…his *daughter* reached out to him…and he slipped his hands around her little body in the sun protective swimsuit while she put her arms around his neck and held on, and heaven help him, but the lump in his throat was so darn huge, he thought he might choke.

"Got her?"

He couldn't look at Cassandra. He swallowed again before answering, "Yeah, I've got her."

He held his daughter…just held her…until she gave a little wiggle and then a giggle…and his heart almost burst through his chest.

"She likes it."

He took a breath and looked up at Cassandra's words. Without warning, something slipped past his guard and bonded with her. It was an odd moment. For the first time he was happy he'd actually married this woman.

She stood up and went to the steps, then slid into the water like a mermaid, dipping under the surface, then coming up in front of Nicole's face. "Boo," she said softly so as not to frighten the little girl.

Nicole blinked, then gave a little squeal of delight and started kicking her chubby little legs, and he needed all his concentration to hold her as she splashed about.

"She's going to be quite a handful," he joked half to himself, but Cassandra smiled back, and for once they were in total accord with this little person linked between them. He veered away from those thoughts. Cassandra couldn't possibly know the very strength of that link.

"Do you want me to take her? She's probably getting heavy by now."

He didn't want to give up holding his daughter just yet. "No, she's fine."

Then Nicole demanded his attention, and he started to walk her slowly around the pool, holding her belly down in the water like she was swimming, her face above the surface. He thoroughly enjoyed playing with her.

Just then he heard Cassandra say something, and he looked up to see her sitting on the lower step of the pool. She was watching them with a soft look in her eyes.

He walked toward her through the water, having completed the circumference of the shallow end of the pool. "Sorry, what did you say?"

"I said I'm glad you're getting to know Nicole."

Wariness rose inside him as he remembered what he had to keep secret. He nodded. "So am I."

Something seemed to catch at her, and she looked down at the water.

His heart thudded. "What's the matter?"

She lifted her head, her eyes sad. "She's so like Liam."

The pain hit him unawares, not because Liam was dead, but because this child in his arms didn't belong to his brother. "*I'm* her father," he ached to say, with an inner pain that had started the day Nicole was born. "*I'm* the one who gave her life."

Instead, he lifted Nicole out of the water and handed her over to her mother. "I've just remembered I have to make a call."

She blinked, a hint of confusion in her eyes as she took hold of Nicole. "Oh, okay."

Then he swept by her up the pool steps, picked up his trousers and shirt and strode inside before he could say something he would regret.

Cassandra wished she hadn't said anything about Liam just now, but Dominic had been such a tower of strength for his family that she'd forgotten mention of his dead brother might sometimes overwhelm him.

Like it had overwhelmed her a moment ago.

Not for her own sake, but for Nicole's.

Her daughter looked so like Liam at times that in spite of everything it hurt to know that he would never get to see his little girl grow up. And that Nicole would never know her father. Sadness swelled in her heart again as the sun went behind a cloud. It felt cooler now out here. Nicole gave a shiver.

She stood up. "Come on, sweetie. Let's get into something warm."

She made her way up the steps to the deck, then went up to her room. There was no sign of Dominic, but his bedroom door was shut and she could hear the shower running. Tension tightened inside her at the thought of all that water dripping down his tanned chest, like it had in the pool. She'd pretended not to notice, but she'd taken a few peeks when he'd been busy with Nicole.

Hurriedly, she closed her bedroom door and put Nicole

on the floor, going over to the wardrobe to get some clothes. It wouldn't do to be thinking about Dominic in the shower, not when he wouldn't be wearing those tight swimmers like she'd seen when he'd left the water. This time he would be naked. Fully naked.

All of a sudden Nicole let out a scream, making Cassandra jump. She rushed forward, seeing her baby's finger caught in the bottom drawer of the bureau, her heart squeezing as Nicole screamed again.

Carefully, she eased Nicole's finger out, relieved to see no blood, then picked her up and cuddled her close. Tears streamed down the baby's cheeks, Nicole's lips trembling as she held on to her mother for solace.

All at once Dominic burst through the door. "What's wrong? What's the matter?"

Cassandra cuddled Nicole against her shoulder. "I left the bottom drawer of the bureau open a little, and she caught her finger."

He came toward them. "Is she all right?"

She nodded, then patted the little back until the crying slowed to sobs. She eased back and picked up Nicole's finger, inspecting it further. There was only a little bit of redness. "Let Mummy kiss it better," she said and placed her lips against the pad of Nicole's finger, love warming the very center of her being. "There. All better now."

As if she were looking for the kiss, Nicole held her finger up in front of her face and frowned. She looked so adorable, with her wet cheeks and pouting lips, that Cassandra shared a smile with Dominic.

"She looks like you," he said, and Cassandra's heart swelled with pride.

A moment later she went to turn away when she caught sight of his chest. His *bare* chest. Taken off guard, her eyes followed the line of dark, silky hair growing down toward his hips, where a towel had been hurriedly thrown around him.

Her bones went soft. Oh, God, what would it be like to run her palms over him?

Would he feel warm and smooth?

Or hot and springy?

Her gaze moved upward to his face—and found him watching her with a hungry expression in his eyes. She self-consciously broke eye contact and looked away, thankful Nicole wriggled to be free at that moment.

Putting her daughter down on the rug, when she looked up, the door was closing behind him on his way out. She sank to the floor in a daze and sat there for several seconds while she caught her breath. The incredible urge to touch Dominic had shocked her with its intensity. What was even more incredible was that if not for Nicole she would have done it.

Four

Dominic had said earlier they would eat alfresco tonight, so Cassandra refreshed her light makeup and gave her shoulder-length hair a quick brush, then smoothed her white cotton shirt down over the matching drawstring pants. Flat sandals gave her outfit a casually elegant look.

Then she went downstairs to find the table on the deck set for two and Dominic standing there dressed in chinos and a shirt, opening a bottle of wine. Behind him the sun was in the midhorizon and slowly sinking in the sky.

It all looked so...romantic.

Her heart jumped in her throat and she had to wonder, would he try and get her into his bed tonight? After the way she'd reacted to him this afternoon, she doubted he'd have to put in much effort.

"Is Nicole asleep?"

"Er...yes." She stepped into the evening and walked toward the table. He met her halfway with a glass of wine, then held out a chair for her. She quickly took her seat before her legs gave way.

Soon he was sitting opposite her and holding up his wineglass in a toast. "Cheers."

She held hers up, too. "Cheers."

He leaned back and took a sip while looking out over the tranquil view of the pool and garden in the bush setting. Cassandra followed his example and could feel a little of the tranquility seeping into her bones.

Dominic turned toward her. "I'm expecting a business call later, but hopefully only after we eat. We're having some problems with a supplier, and I want to keep informed."

She frowned, worried about him for once, though she would never say that to him. "I thought you were going to take a break from work?" was all she said.

"I'm getting plenty of rest," he muttered, the look in his eyes saying that there was rest and then there was *abstinence*.

A quiver pulsed through her veins. "So, what's on the menu?" she said, then thought she could rephrase that better, considering the circumstances.

A flash of amusement said he was thinking the same thing. "I thought we'd eat the seafood from last night."

She felt a stab of guilt for falling asleep like she had. "Good idea, otherwise we'll have to throw it out."

His brow lifted. "Is that the only reason you'll eat it? Would you prefer something else?"

"What? Oh, no. I love seafood. I was just thinking we shouldn't be wasteful."

"Wasteful?" he said as if he'd never heard of the word.

"There *are* starving people in the world, Dominic," she chided, unable to ignore years of her mother's favorite saying.

His mouth tightened. "I know that. It's just something I never expected to hear you talk about."

She bristled at the insult, intentional or not. "Then you don't know me."

A moment crept by.

"I *don't* know you."

"Perhaps it should stay that way," she said, any illusion of ease between them gone, as if it had never been.

His eyes snapped to attention. "What do you mean?"

Everything surged inside her. Fear, tension, the stress of the last few months. "I can't live like this for the rest of our married life, Dominic. No matter what you think of me, I prefer you keep any hostility to yourself in future."

Surprise flickered; then he fixed her with an irritated scowl. "And if I can't?"

She opened her mouth to say that she would leave and get an annulment, but as quickly remembered she couldn't. She was trapped. Dear Lord, she couldn't forget that if he found out about the money for the nursing home, he might put two and two together. Annulment or not, he might still use anything he could find to turn a judge's opinion against her, including Keith Samuels and his convincing lies.

And she could lose Nicole.

Her heart constricted, and she knew she had to appeal to his better nature. It was the only way. It was all she had left.

"Dominic, please. If you can't do it for my sake, do it for Nicole's."

His body tensed. "Nicole?"

"She needs a father. I watched you with her today, and I know you're growing attached to her. Our hostility will only hurt her in the long run."

His face shuttered more than usual, but she had to take

hope that her words would affect him. He wasn't a man who would give in too easily, but surely he would see reason?

"You're right," he finally admitted. "I apologize for my attitude toward you."

Relief whizzed through her, and tears pricked at her eyes. She hadn't expected an apology on top of it all.

Then he added, "Nicole shouldn't have to suffer because of the issues between us."

A dullness hit her at these words, but she quickly put it aside. Fine. So what if his hostility was still just beneath the surface? She shouldn't have expected any different. As long as it didn't affect her daughter, then she could live with it. This was about Nicole, not about herself.

He rose from his chair. "Come on."

Startled, she looked at him. "What?" Was he suggesting they go to bed?

His bemused eyes said he knew she'd jumped to the wrong conclusion. "I need you to help carry out the food."

Was that a stab of disappointment because he *wasn't* talking about making love? She hoped not.

She stood up. "Lead the way."

They carried the food out and sat down to dine on a large platter of king prawns, mussels, salmon rosettes and an avocado filled with delicious marinated calamari. For dessert they enjoyed berry crumble and cream.

Replete, they sat back and sipped at fine wine and watched the sun set over the horizon of trees.

"Are you going to tell your adoptive family about our marriage?" he asked out of nowhere.

Her inner calmness shattered like glass in a mirror. There was really only her sister to tell, but that begged the question. What did Dominic know about her family? Liam had told her that his father had obtained a report on her years ago after their whirlwind marriage. Yet if Dominic was asking now, she assumed there was no updated report. And if that was the case, he wouldn't know that Joe was in a nursing home.

She nodded. "Yes. I'll phone them when we get back to the city," she said, continuing with the pretense. Penny would be hurt if she read it in the papers, but thankfully there was some leeway with that until Dominic released a statement and his parents returned from the cruise. "And by the way, Dominic, they're not just my adoptive family. They're my family. I don't differentiate between the two. I feel just as close to them as I would if they were blood relations."

"You didn't invite them to the wedding," he pointed out.

"And you're surprised?" she scoffed.

He inclined his head, conceding the point. "Would they have come?"

"If I'd asked them to." Penny would have pulled out all the stops to bring her husband and children from Sydney, and would have gotten her family in debt at the same time. Her sister hadn't the money to help out with Joe, either, so she had taken full responsibility for it all from the start. She hadn't minded. She would have found a way to get them here for the wedding if she'd wanted her family here for such a farce. She hadn't.

"So you get on with them?"

She squashed her hurt at the comment. He probably wasn't even aware it implied *she* was at fault. "Yes, we all get on well."

"Tell me about them."

Dangerous ground.

She tried to act casual. "I have a sister. Penny. She lives

in Sydney with her husband and two children." She paused, not sure what to say about Joe. If she said too much—

"And your parents?" Dominic's voice cut into her thoughts. "Your father was ill a few years back, wasn't he?" he said, sending her heart thudding against her rib cage. "I remember my mother mentioning it."

She tried to remain calm and focused. "He was, but he's better now," she fibbed, justifying the lie to herself. "He lives with my sister." Another lie.

"And your mother?"

"She died suddenly about five years ago." Mary had only been sixty and the memory of losing such a loving mother still upset her.

His eyes rested on her, watching her closely. "What happened to your birth parents, Cassandra?"

It was so long ago that she didn't often think about it, but she always felt a twinge of sorrow when she did. "My real mother was killed in a car accident when I was six. My father died when I was nine, but he was gone from me long before that."

He considered her. "I'm sorry. It must have been traumatic for you."

A knot rose in her throat. "Thank you. It was." She appreciated his sympathy.

"But it sounds as if your adoptive family treated you well," he said, like he expected that would be every foster child's lot in life.

"Yes, they did," she was pleased to say.

Yet she had to wonder if a wealthy man such as himself, one who'd been born into privilege like he had, could appreciate how differently things might have gone for her. Did he really understand how it felt for a child to be so alone in the world? Did he know how it felt when there was no one she belonged to anymore? No one to take care of her or protect her? Losing his brother happened to him as an adult. It wasn't the same thing.

"You know, Dominic, they weren't the first family I went to." She saw him give a start. "I was put in another foster home first. I hated it. The 'real' daughter was nasty and used to blame me for everything."

"I see."

Did he?

"Thankfully they found me a new family. I was so lucky to have found the Wilsons," she pointed out. "They'd always been short-term carers, but they were getting on in years and had decided to take in some children with a view to adopting them and giving them their name." Her heart softened. "They were wonderful. They adopted Penny, too, and gave us a family again."

He went still.

His cell phone rang.

She waited, but he didn't move. "That's the call you were waiting for," she prompted gently, noting he looked a little white around the mouth.

"It can wait."

"No, answer it." She'd said all she needed to say.

He looked like he wouldn't move; then he pushed to his feet and strode inside. "Yes?" he barked as he disappeared indoors, and Cassandra rather felt sorry for Adam on the other end of the phone, though she suspected Adam could hold his own against his big brother.

She let out a deep breath, then sat there for a minute, recovering from delving into the past. Part of her knew she'd said more than she should have, but she didn't regret making Dominic more aware of who she really was. At least this way it might be easier for both of them to live with each other. *She* knew where he was coming from. And *he* now knew about her.

Everything except…

She stood and quickly began clearing up, her hands shaking slightly. No, she wouldn't think about her father, the money, or the risk of losing Nicole if Dominic discovered that she'd *sold* her body to her husband to have his baby. Surely life couldn't be so cruel?

And she knew differently.

Taking the dishes inside, she stacked them in the dishwasher and tidied up. She wouldn't think about the past. She had to concentrate on Nicole and giving her daughter the best life she could. And that meant having a mother who didn't let her fears permeate the family unit.

Dominic's low tones on the phone still wafted through the air by the time she'd finished, so she went back out on the deck. Darkness had fallen, and the solar night-lights illuminated the garden. It beckoned her.

She strolled down the steps and past the swimming pool, which was as calm as a millpond right now. It was so beautiful at this time of the evening, with the scent of jasmine in the air. She could feel her shoulders loosening up, the idyllic surroundings sliding the tension right out of her.

"Cassandra, stop!"

She twirled around to see Dominic coming along the path toward her. There was an urgency to his voice. "Wh-what?"

"You're about to walk into a spider's web."

She glanced over her shoulder and saw a huge web strung across the path between two trees. Shuddering, she took a step toward Dominic. "Ugh!"

His arms came out to steady her. "It's okay. I can't see the spider. It's just the web."

"Just?" she choked out, giving another shudder. "I hate spiders."

"I don't particularly like them myself," he said, sounding distracted, and suddenly she saw awareness in his eyes and realized why. Somehow her hands had found their way to his chest. The touch of hard muscle beneath her palms made her tingle.

The air became charged. She forgot the spider. And the web. "I…"

"What?"

Kiss me.

He moved closer. "Cassandra?"

She moistened her lips. "Um…"

He slipped his hands around her waist and brought her up against him. "Say it."

"Kiss me," she whispered.

He groaned as his head came down. Her lips parted on a breath, and she sank into his kiss. *Their* kiss. Their very first kiss as man and woman.

And then his tongue began to stroke hers, dipping inside her mouth with an intoxicating infusion of wine and virility. The sensitive contours flared, and she could feel herself tilting forward into his embrace, sinking farther into him. The intimacy of it turned her upside down. It staggered her to be here in his arms like this.

Then something—she wasn't sure what exactly—revived all her uncertainties and fears. Suddenly it was too much. It all came rushing back. He thought she was a gold digger who'd done his brother wrong. He thought she'd been an unfaithful wife. That she'd had a baby to tie her forever to the Roth family. That it had all backfired on her with the terms of Liam's will. How could he want to make love to her believing that? How could she let him?

"No!" she muttered, jerking away from him.

"What the dev—"

"I'm sorry." She pushed past him and ran inside.

* * *

As hard as it was not to follow her and break down the barriers until she was begging him to make love to her, Dominic let Cassandra go. He didn't want an unwilling woman in his bed. He wanted physical surrender with a willing partner.

God, his body was throbbing with a need he'd held inside him for so long now. She'd tasted so good beneath his tongue, her body tantalizing him as she'd pressed up against him like she had, making him hunger to be inside the very pulse of her. Heat coursed through him at the thought of it.

And clearly she wasn't ready.

He expelled a long breath and forced aside his body's ache, yet that only brought him to what he couldn't ignore.

Her childhood.

His father had requisitioned a report years ago, after she'd married Liam, but he'd never read it himself. What little he'd known about her being adopted, and about her adoptive father suffering a stroke, he'd learned through his family.

But he hadn't been aware it had been so terrible for her. To his shame, he hadn't even thought about her childhood, but now that he had, he couldn't unwind the knot in his gut. It only complicated things now. And heaven help him, things were already complicated more than enough.

Hell, he wasn't unsympathetic. He understood she'd paid a high emotional toll growing up, but he still couldn't get past her marrying his brother for the money, then *staying* married to have a child.

And that made him wonder if her revelation had been deliberate. A sympathy bid? Or more than that? Had she been trying to explain *why* she was a gold digger? Being orphaned had to leave some sort of lasting effect, but was that enough to make what she'd done acceptable? Many other people survived all life had thrown at them without resorting to using people.

He winced. Could he really blame her for wanting more than she had? Did he need to cut her a break about all this?

He firmed his jaw. He had to be careful here. Years ago he'd learned a hard lesson in business, that things sometimes weren't what they seemed. There was always an ulterior motive, always a reason, sometimes valid, sometimes not. He had to consider the possibility that all this openness had merely been a ploy to get his sympathy and win him over.

Cassandra closed her bedroom door and stood listening for sounds of Dominic coming after her, but all was hushed except for the sound of an infant's soft snuffling. Going over to the crib, she was relieved to see Nicole still sleeping.

Then she sank down on the bed and ran her shaky fingers through her hair. Oh, Lord. What had she just done? It wasn't fair of her to lead Dominic on like that, then run away from him. What a thing to do to a man!

To her husband!

Yet would he really have followed her? Already he'd proved he wasn't the type of man to take what *wasn't* on offer. She pulled a face. The thing was, she *wanted* to be on offer. She'd *wanted* him to make love to her right there on the spot.

And then she'd gone and sabotaged herself with her thoughts. She could see now that she'd been overwhelmed by her desire for him. She'd never felt such a deep response before, not even with Liam. With Liam, their lovemaking in the early days had been a pleasant, infrequent flame that had never threatened to flare out of control.

With Dominic, his touch, his kiss, sent hot desire rippling through her veins like lava flowing down a mountain. How could she be a woman who wanted a man she didn't love like her next breath? She would never have believed that would happen to her. She'd always thought she was above sex for sex's sake.

Obviously not.

And clearly she couldn't keep running away from Dominic. Sooner or later she would give in to him. And to her own longings. The thought both thrilled and frightened her.

Right then, the living-room light spilling onto the lawn below her window went off, darkening the bedroom. Her heart surged inside her chest. Was Dominic going to bed now? Would he knock on her door to see if she was okay? Would she answer?

Panicking, she quickly stripped and drew on her silky nightgown, then hopped into bed and pulled the blankets up to her neck. If he looked in, he would think she was asleep.

Then she decided she was such a fool, lying there, listening to nothing. If Dominic was going to bed, he was being very quiet about it. Relaxing at last, she closed her eyes and let herself drift off to sleep.

A sound woke her in the night, and she came awake with a start.

"Cassandra!"

Dominic! It wasn't a yell, but more a loud groan of her name that had reached her through the walls. She threw back the blankets and flew out of bed. Something must be wrong. He'd sounded like he was in pain. Still, mother instinct had her pausing a heartbeat to check Nicole in her crib before she raced out of the bedroom to Dominic's room across the hall.

His door was ajar, and for a moment she stood there, letting her eyes adjust to the room, a sudden thought that an intruder might have gotten through the security system making her breath stall. But no one jumped on her. Nothing moved. She couldn't see any shadows that weren't supposed to be there.

And then Dominic gave a moan, and her gaze sliced to the bed and she saw him lying there, the moonlight falling over him through the open curtains. He moaned again, and her shoulders slumped with relief. He was having a nightmare, that was all. A stupid nightmare.

"Oh, God, Cassandra."

She froze. The huskiness in his voice said he wasn't having a nightmare. He was having a dream.

About her.

Unable to stop herself, she moved forward. He lay on his back, his eyes closed. Her gaze slid slowly downward, past his bare chest to where the blanket had edged to his navel. It was obvious he was fully aroused. Remembering that he was dreaming about *her,* she trembled.

She dragged her eyes back upward. His chest was all muscle, with a light sprinkling of hair, which seemed to beg for her touch. Holding her breath, she reached out. She couldn't seem to help herself.

His skin felt hot and damp, his male scent emanating from him and making her aware of his arousal. She inhaled deeply and grew more bold, the palm of her hand sliding over his flesh.

And then without an inch of warning, his hand trapped hers against him, causing the breath to hitch in her throat. He turned his head toward her; his eyes slid open. For a moment she stood there, frozen. He'd caught her out.

Then he murmured her name, and she realized he was still dreaming. Her heart thudded, not with relief, but with disappointment. She wanted him to pull her into his arms and make love to her without giving her time to think. If she thought too much, she might—

He hauled her into his arms and pulled her on top of him.

The shock of it held her still.

She went to speak, to tell him to wake him up so that he knew what he was doing, but he kissed her, and at that moment she was his. The taste of him, the scent of him, the very feel of him at her thighs were what she wanted most. She didn't have the willpower to pull away from him this time.

And then his hands did a slow march down her body, then up again, as if feeling to make sure she was really in his arms. She knew he was awake then. She broke off the kiss and lifted her head to look down at him.

His dark eyes burned into her. "You're here," he said hoarsely.

She moistened her mouth. "Yes." She swallowed. "I'm staying this time."

In his arms.

He gave a shudder that rippled through her. After that his palms slid over her silky nightgown; then he was lifting it up over her head, taking it off her to give him access to her body. It was so quiet in the room that she heard the sound of the silk dropping to the floor in the sweetest surrender.

"God, I knew you'd be beautiful," he rasped, looking down between them at her firm breasts suspending toward his chest. Then he lifted her higher and held her there while he drew one of her nipples in his mouth.

"Please!" she cried out at the exquisite torture as he tugged the tender bud with his lips, making her arch her neck. But was she asking for more or asking him to stop? She didn't know.

Then he moved to the other breast, and she could feel his erection hard against her lower belly. Sensations of pleasure almost sent her over the edge. Dear Lord, she could never remember being so affected by the touch of a man before. Never had passion overridden everything else. She wanted him so much, she could feel it inside her chest and deep in her bones.

After that everything happened fast. Desire quickly reached the boiling point between them and bubbled over.

With only a pause between breaths, he lifted her by her waist and opened her legs with his own, then eased her over his thickened length, melding their two bodies into one. She wasn't sure which one of them cried out first—maybe both—but one thrust led to another and everything within her started to break free. She abandoned herself around him, feeling him thrust one more time, stiffen and come inside her.

For long moments Cassandra buried her face in his neck while she continued to pulse in rhythm with him. There was a feeling of completeness here she hadn't expected. She and Dominic had become one in the physical sense. And that was more fulfilling than she could ever believe possible.

Something deep in his cells rippled through Dominic as Cassandra's body quieted around him. One minute he'd been dreaming about her; the next he was fully awake and lowering her onto him. He hadn't even taken the time to kiss every inch of her delicious body like he'd imagined he'd do their first time together.

Together.

She stirred above him, lifting her head up from the crook of his neck where she'd collapsed. Moonlight fell across her face at the exact moment she opened her eyes before his, and he saw the pleasure she couldn't hide.

"I was dreaming about you," he murmured, reaching out to brush strands of blond hair off her beautiful face.

She took a breath. "I know." She hesitated. "You called out my name."

Had he?

Yet he wasn't embarrassed. He was proud for her to know he had wanted her so badly.

Still did.

She probably didn't need any further evidence of *that,* he mused, growing hard inside her again. Her eyes widened, filling him with renewed anticipation and making him acutely aware of her wet, silky warmth surrounding him. He groaned, unable to stop his body from giving a brief thrust.

"I've wanted you like this for some time," he managed to say, feeling little clenches of her body, which he knew she couldn't stop.

Her eyes flickered. "Er…you have?"

She was too tempting.

"And you've wanted me," he pointed out, needing to hear her admit what he'd always suspected.

She held his gaze for the longest second, then whispered, "Yes," and lowered her head to his chest, hiding her eyes as if self-conscious.

It sent adrenaline shooting through him, yet at the same time something felt odd. She was showing a sexual vulnerability that didn't tally with what he knew about her. It was like she was only just awakening to passion, and that didn't make sense. She'd had no compunction in having an affair during her marriage to Liam, so why pretend she wasn't experienced?

And then he realized.

Was this just an act? Was it the way she got to a man— making him think he was the only one to tap into hidden sexual depths deep inside her? If it was, then she was very good.

And if it wasn't?

He shook off his thoughts. "Lift your head. Look at me."

"I...don't have the strength."

There it was again.

He rolled them over and reversed their positions. "*Now* look at me."

A heartbeat paused.

She lifted her eyelids.

She was bewitching.

He throbbed with need again and gave another thrust, and all at once she lifted her body to meet him. Triumph raced through him, and he began to move, plunging deeper, thrusting harder. It was incredible that he wanted her again so soon. He'd never known anything like it before.

They came together.

Then his heartbeat slowed, and he eased back to look down on her. She was staring at him with wonder, her eyes telling him she couldn't believe she had climaxed again so soon. He knew the feeling, even as he still wondered about her. For the moment he would take what she offered, give as good as he could get. As long as he remained aware she might be manipulating him, she wouldn't get away with too much.

Then her eyes lowered to his chest, looking away from him again. "We haven't used any protection," she said, her voice barely above a whisper.

His heart lurched in his chest. She wasn't telling him something that hadn't already occurred to him. "It's too late tonight. We'll discuss it tomorrow." He scooped her up in his arms.

"Where are we going?"

"To take a shower together," he said, striding into the bathroom. Standing her on her feet, he reached over and turned on the hot water. "And after that—" he lowered his head for a long kiss and when it had finished, steam was swirling around them "—we're going to start all over again."

Five

Cassandra stretched herself awake to the sound of native bird life, then realized where she was.

In Dominic's bed.

And Dominic was no longer next to her.

She sat up and looked around, blushing when she saw her silk nightgown draped over a chair. The last time she'd seen it, he'd been lifting it over her head.

Oh, my.

The temptation to stay there and relive the night was strong, but she needed to check on Nicole. Peeling herself from under the bedclothes, she grabbed the nightgown to hold in front of her as she crossed the hallway to her bedroom.

No, make that Nicole's room now. Dominic would not let things go back to the way they were.

She had to admit she didn't want that, either. Dare she believe that on another level something else might have changed, too? Could they now be as compatible outside the bedroom as they were inside it?

The crib was empty, and she assumed Dominic had taken Nicole to give her breakfast. And then she heard her daughter's laughter coming from downstairs, and she relaxed. Interested in seeing how he would cope, she quickly took another shower—her stomach giving a little quiver at the memory of showering with Dominic during the night—and then she dressed in a tank top and a tiered skirt that swished about her legs. Hoop earrings made her feel a bit like a gypsy woman.

At the kitchen doorway, it was obvious by the slight mess that Dominic had already fed Nicole her cereal, and now the little girl was happily sitting in her high chair, playing with a selection of her small toys.

He looked up from pouring coffee, his hand stilling. The masculine appreciation in his eyes made her stomach flutter. And the sensuality in them made her tremble. He knew the secrets of her body now. She could not hide from him.

"Good morning," he said huskily.

"Good morning." To cover her blush, she walked toward Nicole, pretending he didn't affect her. "Morning, sweetie," she murmured, kissing the top of her daughter's head, then took a step toward the cupboard to get a coffee mug. She would stay calm, she told herself. She would not panic that he knew how easily she had succumbed to him. Just because—

All at once he was in front of her, pulling her up against his already hard body, reminding her how aroused his dream had made him. Her breath quickened. She could think of nothing more sensual than this man fantasizing about her.

He lowered his head, his mouth closing over hers. She

slid into the kiss like water into a pond. Everything seemed so right between them. So natural.

It couldn't last.

Things never did.

She wasn't sure how long before the kiss ended, but when it did, she quickly stepped around him and went to the cupboard.

"I see you've already fed Nicole," she chatted, not wanting him to know her thoughts. "Thanks for doing that. She would have been hungry."

There was a short silence. Then, "I thought it time Nicole and I got to know each other."

Elation swept through her, the words so sweet.

But as she poured herself a coffee, she admitted that being "sweet" wasn't exactly one of this man's more notable traits. Dominic was renowned for being a shrewd judge of character, in business and out of it—except when it came to *her,* of course.

A moment later she found herself rethinking that. It wasn't just *her* he'd pegged wrong. He hadn't been able to see Liam's true character. In a strange way, such a quality would be endearing if it didn't affect her so much. It showed him to be a caring brother and a protector of his family and—

Unexpected clarity hit her. Last night he'd left his bedroom door ajar. Had that been for a reason? Despite the security alarm being turned on, had he been keeping his ears open in case they needed him? Had he been protecting them?

She grimaced inwardly. Well, protecting Nicole, anyway. He didn't care enough about *her* to want to protect her. As far as he was concerned, she could look after herself. *She* wasn't a true Roth. Not like her daughter was a true Roth.

And that brought her to the heart of the matter. What

more could she ask than he protect her child? It didn't matter that he thought less of her. She could take all he dished out as long as her child was happy and safe. Her daughter being protected at all costs was what mattered most. Dominic's indifference toward her own safety wasn't an issue. She could look after herself. She didn't need his protection or—

She almost dropped the coffeepot as one thought rolled into another, reminding her of another type of protection. One between a man and a woman. One that hadn't been on their minds last night until it was far too late.

"Cassandra?"

She looked up at him and swallowed. "What if I'm pregnant?"

Their eyes collided.

A strange glitter flashed in his eyes before he looked away. "I don't mind."

"You don't?"

His gaze came back at her. "Not yet, of course. But eventually I'd like a couple of children. If it happens now instead, then so be it."

She didn't want it to happen.

She didn't.

Liar.

It was the strangest thing, but the thought of carrying his baby made her feel gooey inside.

And then she realized what that would mean. Having Dominic's baby would tie her to him completely. She'd never be able to get away from him. Somehow with Nicole being his niece and not his own child, it allowed *her* to detach from him in some small way. She'd even thought that sometime in the future, she and Nicole might be able to make a life for themselves without Dominic. But if she became pregnant…if she had *his* child…the ties would be so much more binding. There would be no escape.

Suddenly, the slamming of a car door cut through the silence, followed by another car door closing. Her thoughts subsided as the world intruded.

Dominic frowned, then walked past her into the living room and glanced out the large windows. He swore.

She watched him from the kitchen doorway. "Who is it?"

"We've got visitors."

"Visitors? The housekeeper, you mean?"

"My parents."

Cassandra only just held back a groan as he strode to the front door. Of all the times she didn't want to see her in-laws it was now. It could only mean trouble, she knew, as she went to unbuckle Nicole from the high chair before following Dominic.

"Mum? Dad?" he said as she went to join him at the front door. "What are you doing here?"

His parents were in their late fifties. His father's tallness and handsomeness were the perfect complements to his graceful wife. Both of them came from the best families Down Under. They were true members of the Australian aristocracy. And that made it all the more amazing that they had accepted *her* into their hallowed ranks.

At first.

Laura Roth's face was strained as she looked at her eldest son. Her eyes hardened when she saw Cassandra at his side, and Cassandra's arms tightened around Nicole.

As if Laura noticed the movement, the older woman's gaze slid to Nicole. In an instant, her whole face softened. "Oh, my heavens, Michael," she said, hurrying up the timber steps. "There's our little granddaughter." She held out her arms and Nicole went straight to her. "Take a look at her. She's grown in just a short time. My, she's so like her fath—" Laura burst into tears.

Dominic was the first to move. He quickly lifted Nicole out of Laura's arms, holding on to the little girl himself while his father rushed forward.

Michael pulled his wife into his arms. "Shh, honey. Don't cry."

Cassandra stood there, feeling a deep pang of sadness as her mother-in-law sobbed. No parent should have to lose a child.

"Mum, you shouldn't be here," Dominic muttered, a rough edge to his voice.

Laura sobbed into her husband's chest, but it was Michael who spoke. "We had to come, son," he said, a grave note to his voice, and Cassandra saw Dominic stiffen. Then Michael passed his wife a handkerchief. "Why don't we go inside, honey?"

Laura took a deep shuddering breath and pulled back, wiping her eyes. "I'm fine now, darling. It was just the shock of seeing Nicole." Tears welled up in her eyes again.

"How about some coffee?" Cassandra asked quickly. "Or perhaps something to eat? Have you had breakfast?"

"We had something on the way," Michael said politely, "but coffee would be welcome." He started leading Laura inside.

Cassandra stood there for a moment, then followed them. Dominic was carrying Nicole on his hip, his face closed now. Not a good sign, though for whom she wasn't sure. She winced. Who was she kidding? Dominic's lovemaking last night hadn't changed his opinion of her. Like his parents, he still disliked her.

"I'll put the coffee on," she murmured, once the older couple were seated in the living room. She turned toward the kitchen. It would be a relief to get out of their presence.

"Wait." Michael's abrupt tone stopped her in her tracks. "We have something to say to you and Dominic first."

Cassandra darted a look at Dominic. A muscle ticked in his jaw as he nodded at her, then he put Nicole down in a playpen a few feet away, before going to stand in front of the open fireplace. Cassandra took a seat on one of the armchairs. His parents sat beside each other on the full-length couch, his father holding his wife's hand in his.

"Fire away, Dad."

Michael nodded, a determined look about him. "Right. Well, as you can see we came home early. Last night, in fact. So imagine our incredible surprise when Adam told us about your wedding."

Dominic's mouth compressed. "He should have called to tell me."

"We asked him not to," Michael said. "We wanted to see you in person."

Dominic raised a cool eyebrow. "Why? Is there a problem?"

"Yes, there's a problem," Michael snapped. "Adam told us what was in the will. He said Liam had asked you to do this."

"That's right."

"And that's very commendable of you, son, but your mother and I think you should have waited. There was no need to jump in feetfirst and marry Cassandra. We could have figured out a way around that. Hell, that's what lawyers are for."

Cassandra felt like her breath was cut off. During Liam's illness her in-laws had been cool toward her, but to be so blatant in their loathing of her now was hurtful. Clearly, if

Dominic had married anyone else but her, they wouldn't be here.

Her eyes sought Dominic's, expecting to see the slash of regret now that he knew he should have waited. Strangely, all she could see was a hardness—an intensity—that was surprisingly directed at his parents. The force of it was rather…intimidating.

"There was every need for me to marry Cassandra," he said, his tone brooking no argument.

Michael opened his mouth, then closed it briefly, as if deciding to take a different tack. "Look, we know you did it for Nicole's sake, but—"

"Cassandra and I were both happy to do it," Dominic cut across his father. "Don't doubt that."

"But darling, you could get an annulment," Laura said quickly, making it clear she didn't think they would have already slept together. "We'd be very happy to pay her a lump sum. It would make up for any money she loses from Liam's will."

The words stabbed at Cassandra's heart. It was like she wasn't even in the room, not to mention how much of an insult this was to her. She couldn't take much more from this family.

"So I'm to be a bought woman now?" she exclaimed, jumping to her feet.

"Aren't you that already?"

Cassandra sucked in a sharp breath. "I can't believe you said that, Laura."

Laura at least had the grace to wince. "I—"

"Enough," Dominic snapped in a low, harsh voice. "Mum, Dad, listen to me. Cassandra is *my* wife now whether you like it or not. I suggest you learn to accept it or—"

"Or what, son?" Michael faced him off.

Two strong men.

Dominic's eyes darkened dangerously. "Don't force me to make a choice, Dad. Nicole is our main concern. If you want to be a part of her life, then you'll have to learn to live with her mother."

There was a moment's shocked silence.

Laura's face twisted with anguish. "But she turned Liam against us, Dominic. And now she's turning *you* against us, as well."

Cassandra gasped. "I didn't. I'm not," she mumbled, stunned, seeing Dominic give her a slight shake of his head, telling her to stay out of this. Oh, God. Wasn't she even allowed to defend herself against these people?

"It might be a good idea for you to go make the coffee," Dominic suggested.

"But—"

"Make the coffee, Cassandra," he said firmly. "Please."

It was the *please* that did it. She glanced briefly at Nicole playing happily in the playpen, then left the room, unable to look at the others. She couldn't.

In the kitchen she refilled the coffeepot and turned it on, her movements automatic. Then she went to the sliding patio door and stood looking out over the swimming pool. She could hear the murmur of voices coming from the living room, but she didn't want to know. It was clear what they all thought of her.

It hadn't always been this way between them. That was the hardest part to take. If they'd been against her from the beginning, instead of making her feel like a part of the family... If she hadn't fallen in love with them on sight... then this wouldn't be so hard to take now. She loved Laura and Michael, and now she felt betrayed by them.

Worse, it was apparent they reciprocated the feeling.

They blamed her for many things, and *she* could only blame Liam for that. Liam, who'd been jealous of her relationship with them from the start. Liam, who'd later taken every opportunity to twist things around to make her look bad. Liam, who'd wanted her to have his baby, then shunned her and Nicole when he insisted on going home to die. And finally, Liam who'd forced her to marry his brother.

To give Nicole a Roth upbringing?

Or to make *her* life a misery?

"Is the coffee ready yet?"

She spun around. "What! Oh, yes."

Dominic stared at her across the width of the kitchen, some sort of indefinable emotion in his eyes. "Are you okay?"

"Of course." She stood there, trying to compose herself. It wasn't easy pushing her thoughts aside when she'd just been knocked down so hard by his parents.

"I'm sorry about what they said back there."

She blinked. She was grateful he'd stood up to his parents, she really was, but it hadn't been for *her* benefit at all. Not even a little bit. Dominic had made love to her last night, but he really hadn't changed his opinion of her. She doubted he ever would.

She angled her chin, aware that staying angry helped her to cope. "Why? It's only what you were thinking yourself."

His mouth tightened. Those blue eyes of his turned cold. "Whatever I think isn't important right now. I married you, Cassandra, and we're going to stay married. So let that be the end of it."

Her insides ached at the circumstances that had brought them to this. She had to accept that her situation wasn't going to change.

She gave a sharp nod. "I'll be there shortly."

He held her gaze a moment more, then turned and left the room. Somehow she made herself move. She had to make the coffee and she had to walk back in that living room and face far more hostility than she'd ever imagined. Ye Gods! What had she ever done to deserve this?

Then she remembered Nicole. Forced to marry Dominic or not, she *had* done the right thing for her daughter. Nicole *would* have her birthright. Nicole *would* be raised a Roth. And if Liam's intention had been to make her own life a misery because of it, then she would cope.

She always had.

She always would.

When she came back in the living room, Laura gave a stiff smile. "I'd like to apologize for what I said before, Cassandra. I was out of line."

She almost dropped the tray of coffee. Cassandra exchanged a quick glance with Dominic, aware he would have put his mother up to this. All the same, just this small thing made her feel better. "Thank you, Laura."

"I was out of line, too," Michael added, a tight look about his features that reminded her of Dominic. "I'd like to apologize, as well."

Cassandra tried to give an impersonal nod. "Thank you, Michael," she said, but she was glad she could occupy herself with handing out the coffee. She didn't want them to see the tears pricking the back of her eyes. She yearned to be friends with them again, but that was something she couldn't let them see.

Once they were all settled with their coffee, it was Dominic who spoke first. "So, Dad, what are your plans for the rest of the day?"

His father gave a half smile. "Are you trying to get rid of us, son?"

Dominic gave an equally short smile. "Not at all. I was merely going to ask if you wanted to stay for lunch."

Michael shook his head. "Thank you, but your mother and I need to head back to Melbourne shortly."

Just then, Nicole babbled something and everyone's head swiveled toward the playpen, where her daughter played happily with her toys. She looked so cute that Cassandra's heart surged with love.

"Oh, look at that little poppet," Laura said, putting her cup down on the coffee table. "I have to give her a cuddle. I—" The older woman went to get to her feet, turned pale, then sat back down.

"Mum?" Dominic got to his feet.

Michael leaned closer to his wife. "Honey, you've lost all color."

Laura put out a hand, taking a moment to speak. "I'm fine. I just felt faint all of a sudden."

"Are you sure?" Michael asked, frowning.

She swallowed. "Don't fuss, darling. I'm okay."

"You've got some color back now," Dominic said, studying her with concern. "Things have been too much for you, Mum. I insist that you both stay here overnight before heading back to Melbourne."

"Oh, but—"

"No *buts*. You've just driven over two hours to get here. You don't need to turn right around and go straight back."

"Dominic's right," Michael said. "I think it may be too much for you. And for me, too, seeing we didn't bring our chauffeur," he added for good measure. "Besides, we did bring an overnight bag in case we decided to stay somewhere."

Laura bit her lip. "But we don't want to intrude."

"You won't be intruding," Cassandra heard herself say,

knowing she honestly couldn't send her mother-in-law away when the woman wasn't feeling well. "There's more than enough bedrooms."

Tears welled in Laura's eyes. "Thank you," she murmured.

Michael looked relieved, his eyes softening a little as he looked at Cassandra. "Yes, thank you."

Cassandra's heart wobbled as she inclined her head. Then she pushed aside sentimentality as she realized her in-laws hadn't expected her and Dominic to have shared a bed last night. She'd be embarrassed if they found out otherwise right now.

"I'll just go upstairs and find a suitable room for you both," she said, not looking at Dominic as she left them to it and hurried up the stairs.

First, she needed to make sure she hadn't left any of her clothes lying around his room. Of course, Laura and Michael must accept eventually that she and Dominic would share a bed. Just not now. Heck, maybe Dominic wouldn't want her to share his bed again, anyway. She'd been assuming he would. Both thoughts caught at her breath.

The larger bedroom farthest away would be perfect for the older couple. And the only thing in Dominic's room to show she'd been there was the imprint of two heads on the pillows. She hurriedly tidied the bedclothes, trying not to think about being in Dominic's arms.

She was quietly closing his door, when she turned around and he was there behind her in the hallway. She jumped.

"Looking for something?" he said silkily.

Her heart started to race. "Er…no. I was just making sure—"

"That there was no incriminating evidence?"

She could feel a blush rising up her neck. "If you like."

The tension in the air shot up like a thermometer. "Oh, yeah, I like," he murmured, moving an inch closer.

"Dominic, I—"

A noise downstairs broke the moment, and that was just as well. Dominic was such a powerful lover that she wanted to be in his arms again. She was melting so fast where he was concerned. She needed to step back and put some sort of distance between them. He was getting too close and she was in real danger of letting him become more than she should want.

Thankfully he had a remote look about him now. "I just came to say thank you for encouraging my parents to stay."

"It was the right thing to do."

"You could have sent them to a motel."

"No." It hadn't occurred to her, and she wouldn't have done that even if it had.

"You were nicer to them than they deserved."

The comment surprised her. "They're Nicole's grandparents. I have to be."

"No. You don't."

Her brows drew together. "Whose side are you on, Dominic?"

There was a longish pause.

"No one's," he said curtly, then turned and walked away.

The housekeeper came later that morning to give the place a tidy up, bringing a selection of fresh food and supplies. By this time, Laura felt better and she suggested they go into town to buy a couple of things she hadn't brought with her for an overnight stay.

So they drove the short distance into Lorne and took a stroll around the town. Then they had lunch in one of the finer restaurants, but not before Cassandra took the opportunity to buy a one-piece swimsuit, aware she'd be too embarrassed to wear her skimpy bikini in front of his parents.

Once they were back home, Laura insisted on carrying her granddaughter up the stairs when Cassandra went to put Nicole down for her afternoon nap. She couldn't help but notice the satisfied look in her mother-in-law's eyes when it was obvious she was sharing a room with Nicole, not Dominic.

But thankfully Laura said nothing about it, and soon they'd changed into their swimsuits and joined the men poolside. It should have been relaxing in the summer sun. But that wasn't remotely close to how she was feeling, Cassandra decided, watching Dominic come up the steps of the pool, water dripping from him. She tried not to look, but there was something sexy about a man all wet and awash. She'd learned that last night in the shower. She went all goose-bumpy at the thought.

And then she looked into Dominic's eyes before he slipped his sunglasses back on, and she knew there was something just as sexy about the way a man looked at a woman he found attractive. Her pulse raced as his gaze briefly slicked down over her sea-green one-piece as she lay on the lounger. Amazingly, her swimsuit had looked rather demure inside the boutique, but in front of Dominic the outfit shouted "seduce me." She suspected he would have, too, if his parents hadn't been there.

The rest of the afternoon dragged on, though there were moments when everyone was surprisingly pleasant. Nicole was the common thread between them all, and once the little girl woke up, her grandparents were delighted to spend time fussing over her.

Eventually, Laura tired and took a nap, while Dominic and Michael played chess and kept an eye on Nicole so that Cassandra could prepare the dinner. But as the sun sank in the distance, she could feel the tension escalating inside Dominic. It was spine-tingling to know he wanted her, but she had to keep her own feelings of desire under control. She knew he wouldn't make love to her tonight with his parents in the house, but what about tomorrow after they left? Would he still want her then? Would she want him? God help her, but the answer was yes!

Later, they watched a movie, then Laura and Michael retired for the night. Cassandra decided she couldn't stay downstairs with Dominic, so she yawned and said she was going to bed, too.

He got to his feet. "I'll come check on Nicole with you."

She blinked. "Oh...okay."

The air hopped with sensuality as they went up the stairs. She could feel it in every step they took, but he didn't say a word as they stood over the crib and looked down at the sleeping infant. Then he lifted his head and looked at *her,* and Cassandra held her breath as his eyes moved over her face. She suspected he was about to kiss her good-night.

He spun away with a jerky movement and walked back to the door. "Good night," he rasped.

She stood there, swallowing her disappointment, but aware this was for the best. "Good night." She went to bed.

A restless night followed. She kept imagining Dominic in his bed across the hallway, tossing and turning, thoughts of the previous night in his mind. So it was sweet revenge to see the dark circles under his eyes the next morning when she entered the kitchen with Nicole. At least she wasn't the only one to feel tired and tense.

Laura and Michael were already there and they both looked rested. They fussed over Nicole, but once things settled down and they'd finished eating, their attitude toward Cassandra took on a slight chill again. It was as if having to go back to Melbourne reminded her in-laws of everything wrong she'd "supposedly" done to Liam. Her heart cramped with the unfairness of it. She couldn't win. Not with Dominic. Not with her in-laws.

The older couple left midmorning, kissing Dominic and Nicole goodbye, but managing to avoid kissing her, so it was with a mix of relief and despair that she stood watching their car go down the driveway. She doubted she'd be afforded a peck on the cheek by them ever again.

Dominic shifted beside her, and thoughts of her in-laws faded from her mind. She and Dominic were now the only adults here for the rest of the week. Would he make love to her? There was nothing to stop him.

Then Nicole squirmed in her arms.

Nothing…except Nicole.

"I have some work to do in the study," he muttered, turning to go back inside. He stopped. "Will you and Nicole be okay?"

She was surprised he asked. She nodded and said, "Yes."

An hour later, Dominic still hadn't put in an appearance. Cassandra had tidied up the kitchen and played with Nicole, but now it was her daughter's nap time. She put her down in the crib, then decided to go downstairs and read by the pool. First, though, she changed out of her summery dress into a pair of shorts and a halter top, not quite brave enough to change into her bikini or one-piece suit.

Five minutes later she padded out on the patio and sank down on the lounger. She was aware that Dominic had seen her from the study, where she'd caught a glimpse of him standing at the window, talking on his cell phone. She'd felt the impact of his gaze even at this distance.

She opened her book and pretended to read, not that she was taking in any of the words now. Her heart was pounding and the pages were a blur. Dominic had made her *his* the other night and his look just now told her he wanted her again. She was weak, but, oh, she wanted him again, too. It had been building since yesterday morning.

Ten minutes later he still hadn't come outside. Had she imagined that look from the window? she wondered, pushing to her feet and going to the kitchen to see what they could have for lunch.

She was looking in the refrigerator when she heard a noise behind her. Straightening, she turned around. Dominic was standing in the doorway. His eyes were filled with hot desire. He didn't say a word as he came toward her—and made straight for her lips.

His kiss was white-hot, plundering her mouth like he'd been starving for her forever. It was a mind-numbing experience having a man devour her like this, wanting her this much, his tongue painting her with his taste.

Velvet on velvet.

He pushed her back against the coolness of the refrigerator and began kissing nibbles the length of her collarbone to the curve of her shoulder. She inhaled the faint citrus aftershave he wore. Combined with his own scent, it went straight to her head.

Then his lips made their way back and she turned her head slightly before he could reach her, ready to meet his mouth with her own, offering it to him. He took her in one swoop.

She could feel his hands roaming over her, but it wasn't until he broke off the kiss to look down at her lace-cupped breasts that she realized he'd undone the halter tie at her neck. Her top had slipped to her waist, leaving her standing there in her strapless black bra, and in the clear light of day, his masculine eyes took in every detail.

"You're beautiful," he said huskily, unhooking her bra, and she spilled into his hands. She gave a soft moan as he cupped her, his thumbs skimming across her nipples, budding them until they ached for more. His fingers obliged, taking the brown peaks and rolling them until she tingled all the way down to her toes. It was the most superb form of punishment.

His hands left her breasts and she wanted to cry out not to stop, but they merely slid down to her waist and pushed her halter top farther down her hips. Using the same skimming movement that he'd done to her nipples, he skimmed his thumbs over her hips and oddly, it was just as intense. His eyes held hers, watching her face.

She felt his fingers go under her shorts, pushing them down as his whole body sank downward, too, pushing all her clothes off her, including her high-cut panties, exposing her to him.

Her heart stood still for a moment.

She watched him move his head toward her stomach and place his lips against her belly button. She gasped, but that was nothing compared to the gasp she gave as he began placing little kisses down to the V at her thighs.

One by one.

She moistened her mouth. "Um…what are you doing?"

He gave her his answer. In next to no time he had her melting under his tongue.

Velvet fire.

Six

For the rest of the week they took time out to walk along some of the beaches in the area and visited the beautiful waterfall at Erskine Falls. They also drove along the Great Ocean Road to Apollo Bay, then a little farther on to Cape Otway to visit one of Australia's oldest lighthouses. In the evening they watched movies or played cards or chess.

Dominic had been right that this break would do her good. In spite of the tension between them, now that she was away from the city and all the reminders of Liam, she felt a little less stressed as each day passed by.

Dominic seemed more laid-back as well though sometimes she'd catch him staring at her with a withdrawn look about him. She didn't have to wonder why. His opinion of her hadn't changed. Not really. He might understand her a little more now he knew about her upbringing, but in his eyes that didn't excuse her for being a gold digger, nor for her supposed affair. And he was still angry with her for the way he thought she'd treated Liam. He wasn't about to let go of those feelings.

She had to admit she hadn't cared so much before what he thought. She'd had too much else on her mind with Nicole and Joe, and had tried not to think about her and Dominic's future together. Now it hurt. Somewhere down the track she'd imagined he would see past all the issues between them and would even come to like her, not just want her body. Only, he *was* seeing past the issues and he still didn't like her much. It didn't give her hope for a promising future.

Finally, the "honeymoon" was over, and they left for Melbourne on Monday morning. The holiday had been a lovely and much-needed break, but the closer they got to the city, the more Cassandra could feel the pressures rising between her and Dominic.

There were so many things they would have to deal with now, not the least of which was Christmas in less than two weeks. It would be a sad holiday for the family this year, and she hadn't even reminded anyone it was her birthday on Thursday. She was happy to let it pass. It didn't seem right to be celebrating at a time like this.

And there was the media to face, though thankfully Michael had been able to use his connections to keep news of her and Dominic's marriage low-key. The media weren't usually so kind, and their response said a lot about the high regard the country held for the family.

Of course, she still had to call her sister, Penny, then go sort out everything at the nursing home. She'd do that tomorrow, after Dominic went back to work. She just prayed that her share of Liam's estate would be there without her having to ask Dominic. So far, nothing had gone into her bank account.

They arrived back at Sandringham at noon. Nesta welcomed them, then went about the business of unpacking their luggage while Dominic took Cassandra and Nicole on a tour of their new home.

It was a dream mansion and impressed Cassandra in every way it could. There was a sparkling kitchen and modern furniture throughout. Expansive glass in the living room overlooked stunning gardens. A pool and a tennis court begged to be used, and the place even had a fully equipped gym.

Upstairs, the bedrooms, designed for luxury, were en suite and the master bedroom had a private balcony with a view of the bay. And she only had to look into Dominic's eyes to know they would make full use of the spa bath.

Her cheeks felt warm as they went back downstairs, but had cooled by the time they sat down to eat a late lunch. After that, Nicole had her afternoon nap, while Dominic needed to go into the city to speak to Adam at the office. Nesta hurried off to prepare dinner.

And suddenly Cassandra was alone.

It struck her then. This was it. This was her life now. They were back in the real world, and nothing was going to change for her. She'd still be a trophy wife, and now another husband would be busy with his work. Just like it had been with Liam until he became ill. Liam had been a very social person and she'd at least kept herself occupied arranging all his parties. Dominic was more private. She wasn't sure what he expected of her in this regard.

Unnerved, she knew she couldn't while away the hours doing nothing. She loved being a mother and spending time with Nicole, but this time she needed something for herself, even if it was only a couple of hours a week.

Something.

Anything.

A part-time job? Volunteer work? She didn't even have a car to get around in, Liam having insisted on supplying a driver whenever she'd needed one. It hadn't changed after his illness had been diagnosed. In fact, having a driver had been a blessing with all the medical appointments and then the visits to see him at his parents' house.

She took a deep breath and told herself not to panic. She wasn't trapped inside this house for good. There were ways around things. She had four hundred dollars in the bank, and that at least could pay for a few cab trips to go see her father until the money started flowing again once the will was finalized. Then she would buy herself a car. And she would find a responsible babysitter for Nicole, or perhaps Nesta would babysit a couple of times a week. The housekeeper was a widow and had a couple of grandchildren herself.

As for today, suddenly she had the strongest urge to go to her old home. Everything had been so rushed last week that she'd walked out the door the morning of the wedding without even a last look around.

She was about to reach for the phone to call a cab when she remembered Dominic's Porsche. Of course! Did he still have it? She hurried to check if it was there. It was. Dare she? He might even allow her to use it in the future, though she wouldn't hold her breath. Men were funny when it came to their cars.

"I'm not sure this is a good idea," the housekeeper fretted when Cassandra told her she wanted to go for a drive and asked her to keep an eye on Nicole, who was sleeping. She wasn't one to dump her daughter on anyone, but she badly needed to get out of the house right now.

"Why not? It's a beautiful day, and I want to have a look around the area by myself." She and Liam had lived quite a few suburbs away.

Nesta reluctantly gave her the keys. "Okay, but promise me you'll call me if you need anything."

"I promise. Look, here's my cell number so that you can call me if need be." She wanted to be in contact in case Nicole needed her, and Nesta seemed happy with that.

The Porsche was a beautiful car, and for a split second she sat in it in the double garage and hesitated about driving it. Then she remembered how Dominic had gone off to the office and done his own thing this afternoon, so why couldn't she? Anyway, she'd take it easy.

By the time she'd driven out the automatic gates, she was getting the hang of driving again. She'd forgotten how being in control had felt, especially with such a sleek, powerful car under her hands. After a while she even turned up the radio and let the breeze whip her hair, and by the time she reached her old house, some of the cobwebs in her mind had been blown away.

The first thing she saw as she pulled up in front of the town house was a For Sale sign. It took her by surprise and sent a shock of anger through her. Damn him. Dominic didn't muck around. It had been only a week since she'd left.

Feeling almost like an intruder, she parked in the driveway. Some mail was sticking out of the letterbox, so she emptied it, *not* surprised there wasn't a birthday card from Penny. Her sister had never been one to send cards or letters, but Cassandra knew she cared and that was all that mattered.

Then she walked up to the front door, half expecting her key not to fit the lock, but it did and she went inside to find nothing had changed. *Nothing except her,* she thought, walking into the living room and seeing all the furniture still there.

Then she realized something, and she was shocked

to see there were no personal items left in the room. No doubt Dominic had arranged to have them stored away somewhere, but it was typical of his high-handedness that he hadn't even told her.

She took a couple of steps toward the kitchen to check the rest of the house, but all at once her anger was replaced by an odd feeling and her feet wouldn't move past this point.

She simply didn't want to walk into the kitchen, where she'd organized many a dinner party for Liam's friends and business acquaintances, and where Keith had forced his attentions on her until Liam had walked in. Or go inside the bedroom she'd shared with Liam, and certainly not the spare bedroom he'd moved into after he'd started his intensive treatment before going home to die.

The whole house had a defeated air about it, despite the brightness of the white decor, which Liam had chosen. Or perhaps it was just the sad and unhappy memories here. More than likely that was it, she admitted, giving one last look around before truly saying goodbye to Liam in her heart and walking out the front door.

She now had closure.

Nesta looked greatly relieved to see her, and Cassandra had to admit that having a welcoming face meet her at the door made her feel slightly cherished. Cassandra then spent the rest of the afternoon "cherishing" her little girl in turn.

Dominic returned around seven and she was tempted to tackle him about the arrogant way he'd dealt with the house and personal belongings, but Nicole had been fed and bathed and was getting grumpy. But when he took the time to put her daughter on his lap and play with her for a few minutes, Cassandra's anger at him lessened, and then her heart melted watching the two of them together.

If anything happened to her, Nicole would be loved and cared for. She was so grateful for that.

It wasn't until he gave Nicole a good-night kiss, then went off to take a shower, that Cassandra remembered she should have called Penny. It was too late now with Dominic in the house, so it would have to wait until tomorrow. And that would work out even better, she decided. She could visit her father first, then give her sister an update.

"If you want to change anything about the place," Dominic said over dinner, "then let me know."

Change anything?

"No, this place is perfect." And that reminded her... "By the way, I went for a drive this afternoon."

He went still. "A drive?"

Ooh, she was going to enjoy paying him back. "In your Porsche."

"My Porsche? What the hell!"

"Don't worry. I didn't damage it." She deliberately bit her lip. "Of course, I *did* come rather close to that bus." She wrinkled her nose. "But no, there were a few inches left between us by the time I slammed on the brakes."

There! Go smoke that in your pipe, Mr. Roth.

He muttered a curse. "I don't give a damn about the car. There are people out there who don't have any scruples about who they hurt, let alone a woman with a small child."

Her amusement instantly vanished. She hadn't thought of that. "I didn't take Nicole. Nesta looked after her."

His mouth tightened. "A woman by herself or with a child makes no difference to some. You put yourself in danger."

Was he just trying to frighten her to keep her on some sort of leash? "That's a bit overkill, isn't it?"

"No. Don't you remember six months ago when that

wealthy woman was kidnapped and killed by a disgruntled employee of her husband's? And the gem dealer who was killed in a bungled robbery a month ago? I don't think their families would say it was overkill, do you?"

A flutter of fear went through her, but she tried to ignore it. "I can't live in an ivory tower, Dominic."

"You don't have to. If you want to drive the Porsche, then we'll do it on the weekend together, but if you need to go out during the week, I'll have my driver take you." He stopped, his eyes resting firmly on her. "Promise me, Cassandra, or I'll put a tail on you."

"A ta-tail?" she stuttered.

"A bodyguard."

Her heart jumped in her throat. If he did that, then she wouldn't be able to visit her father. She couldn't let that happen. "No one worried about any of this before I married you. I could come and go as I pleased."

"Things have changed. All our drivers are trained to protect the family now."

"Good Lord," she muttered. The real possibility of something happening to any of them, but especially to her baby, made her feel sick.

"Look, it's nothing to be too stressed over," he assured her, his tone mellowing. "The world's getting to be a dangerous place and we're simply not taking any chances. Go about your business, but be aware of what goes on around you." He paused. "It wouldn't be nice for Nicole to lose her mother now, would it?"

Thud.

So this was about him being alarmed over Nicole's welfare, not her own. She really was grateful he was thinking about her daughter, but just once it would have been nice to be included in his concern.

Suddenly, his lack of concern for her was the catalyst

she needed to stop her guilt over visiting Joe. She'd begun to feel bad about the lies she'd have to tell, but now...

"Does this mean I can't keep my appointment with my dentist tomorrow?" she said, the excuse popping into her head. "I made it weeks ago."

His eyes sharpened. "My driver will take you wherever you want to go. If he's not available, there are others on hand."

"I don't want to put anyone to any trouble."

"It's no trouble," he said coolly, but she could feel him watching her with an unexpectedly intense look.

Then she understood why. He was distrustful of her motives. He probably suspected she was going to meet a lover. God, it still hurt that she'd never been able to convince Liam of the truth. And now his brother had taken up the baton.

Ignoring the pain in her heart over being wrongly accused, she continued eating her meal, aware she'd have to be doubly careful tomorrow. Somehow she'd have to give the driver the slip. It wasn't going to be so easy....

Of course! Her dentist was in the city center in one of the many arcades. She could get the driver to drop her off where there was no parking. If by some chance he came looking for her, she'd say she'd gotten her appointments mixed up and had gone shopping instead. And if Dominic challenged her about it later, she would deal with it then.

"So," Dominic said, leaning back in his chair after Nesta took away their plates and while they were waiting for dessert. "Did you go anywhere in particular on your drive?"

All at once her anger rose inside her again. She glared at him. He was so damn arrogant. "To my old place. I see you're selling it."

"There's no reason not to." His mouth drew down at the corners. "Is there?"

"That's not the point. The dust hasn't settled on our marriage and you've already put the house on the market. And you pack up all my and Liam's personal belongings and take them somewhere without even asking me."

"Your personal belongings are in one of the spare rooms here in this house, until such time as you want to sort through them."

Not good enough.

"You could have waited. I might have liked to do it myself."

"I thought I'd save you the trouble."

She wouldn't say thank-you. She just wouldn't.

He studied her. "You know, I used to think that house suited you and Liam, but now I realize it didn't suit you at all. It was Liam it suited."

As crazy as it was, a slither of pleasure made its way past her anger. Was he starting to see her as she really was? As quickly, she realized she was fooling herself. Dominic saw only what he wanted to see.

She pretended indifference. "That's because Liam chose the furnishings."

"Why?"

She blinked. "Why?"

"Why did Liam choose them? Why didn't *you* choose them? I'd think a new wife would have wanted to incorporate her own ideas and designs in her new house."

"You've already got your answer. It was Liam's house and Liam chose the designs."

He scowled at her. "It was your house, too."

She shook her head. "No, it wasn't, Dominic. Liam bought it with his money and it was in his name. He even deeded it over to you, remember?"

"I remember, but I'm talking about more than owning the house. I'm talking about both of you being a husband and wife in that house."

"So am I."

His eyes closed in on her. "Is that why you had an affair?"

"Wh-what?"

"You heard me."

She shook her head. She couldn't let him get away with this. It was important she stand up for herself. "No. I told you. There *was* no—"

Just then Nesta returned carrying dessert, and Cassandra quickly swallowed back her words. The housekeeper didn't appear to notice anything out of the ordinary as she took their empty plates and passed on a message that Adam wanted Dominic to call him back after dinner.

Once they were alone again, Cassandra waited, but Dominic didn't resume his questioning. He did shoot her a dark look and she knew he wouldn't believe anything she said anyway, so she was grateful when he ate his dessert then excused himself.

She could kick herself now for discussing anything about her marriage to Liam with him. She and Dominic weren't friends. Sometime in the future he may well find out what Liam had really been like as a husband and that she'd never had an affair, but right now she was risking everything by giving information away to a man who thought she slept around. Information he could well use against her.

She had to remember she didn't want his team of lawyers investigating her marriage to Liam. Not now. If ever. In six months' time, the lawyer would destroy that letter Liam had written accusing her of blackmailing him into having his baby. Then there would no longer be any written evidence to support her late husband's "truth" that she'd blackmailed him. And that meant there would no longer be written "evidence" that she'd had an affair with Keith Samuels.

Unfortunately, it still wouldn't be enough to set her free. Liam had told his brother about her and Keith, painting her an unfaithful wife so that Dominic could use it against her in court if need be. She had no doubt he would.

Seven

The next morning at ten, Cassandra left Nicole with Nesta and had Dominic's driver drop her off outside one of the beautifully restored shopping arcades in the city. There were a few tense moments when he wanted to wait for her, but she assured him she would be a couple of hours and would call him when the treatment was finished. Then she left via another exit and caught a cab to visit her father. Joe didn't always recognize her. He did today.

"Cassie, how lovely to see you," he said, sitting on the bench in the nursing home garden as she walked toward him.

She gave him a hug and a kiss and blinked back silly, soppy tears. "Dad, it's good to see you, too."

"What are the tears for?"

"I'm just happy to see you." She sat down on the bench next to him.

"Me, too. How's Nicole? You didn't bring her today?"

"She had the sniffles, so I thought it best she stay home." Dominic would have been suspicious if he'd learned she'd taken Nicole with her to the "dentist."

"And Liam? How's he doing? He must be working really hard. I haven't seen him for a long time."

Her heart sank at the clear indication her father wasn't getting better. She'd already gently explained to him that Liam had been very sick, though she hadn't yet told him that he'd died. Perhaps in this case there was no need to do that when he probably wouldn't remember, anyway.

"He's still working hard. He sends his love." Liam had always been too busy and had met Joe only a couple of times; once before their marriage and once afterward. Then both men had gotten sick.

Her father frowned. "He does?"

For a second she wondered if he'd heard about Liam's death on the television or the radio.

"Your mother will be sorry she missed you."

"Wh-what? You spoke to Mum?" she asked cautiously. This was worse than she thought.

"Yes."

"Where is she now?"

He glanced around and his eyes started to cloud over. "Somewhere." There was a flare of panic in them. "I don't remember."

"That's okay, Dad." She patted his twisted hand, which had never recovered from the stroke. "Why don't you and I sit and enjoy the sunshine for a while. It's so nice out here."

He took a shaky breath and nodded.

She stayed to chat for another fifteen minutes, until it was their early lunchtime. Then she walked her father inside and sat him down at the table with the others and said goodbye, her heart heavy. She hated seeing her dad like this. It didn't seem fair. He'd given so much to the community in caring for foster kids, and then by adopting her and Penny, though he'd always said he and Mum had received so much in return.

She sniffed back some tears as she went in search of the nursing home administrator. As she was walking down the hallway, a sudden noise made her jump and she saw an elderly woman had knocked her tray of food on the floor of her room. Cassandra hurried to move her out of the way before the woman slipped and injured herself.

One of the staff came rushing in. "Thank you so much! I was trying to get back to help feed Rose, but one of the other patients was sick." She shook her head. "It's a pity there aren't two of me here today."

At that moment a thought clicked in Cassandra's mind. Was it possible for her to do volunteer work here at the nursing home? Not only would she be able to see her father without Dominic knowing, but something felt so right about helping these elderly people. It felt good.

She left the room, excitement running through her veins as she headed to the administrator's office. She'd sort out the money problem, then ask about volunteering.

"Mrs. Roth," the administrator said, getting to her feet as Cassandra entered her office. "I'm glad you're here. I was going to call you."

Cassandra put up her hand to stop her before she said anything further. "I know what you're going to say, Jane. I'm late with this month's payment."

Jane Clyde gestured for her to take a seat. "Yes, and I'm sorry to bring it up right now, Mrs. Roth, but it's my job to make sure no one gets too far behind in their payments. It makes it difficult when we have to deal with the problem in a somewhat…harsh way." She gave a sympathetic look. "Is there any way I can help?"

Cassandra swallowed hard. With lawyers and wills, it could be months before the money was all sorted if she didn't put pressure on them to hurry it up. She had to speak to Dominic as soon as possible.

"Jane, I'm sure you'll understand that it's been a traumatic time for me, but I assure you that my late husband's estate is being finalized as we speak. I should be getting the money very soon," she said, crossing her fingers.

Jane smiled with relief. "That's fine then, Mrs. Roth. And by the way, I want to congratulate you on your new marriage." Her face turned serious. "And of course I want to say how sorry I am about your late husband."

Cassandra became conscious that her hurried remarriage must look peculiar to this woman, yet there was nothing in Jane's demeanor to reflect anything but good wishes.

"Thank you. And please, I've told you before to call me by my first name."

Jane merely smiled. "Thank you, but I couldn't."

Cassandra shook her head in exasperation. It was because of the family name. People tended to think that because she was a member of the Roth family, she should be afforded some sort of deference. As if *Roth* and *royal* were synonymous. She grimaced inwardly. Of course, in Australian society circles they were.

And now they had that out of the way...

"Jane, I was wondering. Do you need any volunteers here at the nursing home?"

The other woman's eyes widened in astonishment. "Are you talking about *yourself?*"

"Yes. I'd love to help out here a couple of days a week. I can clean, cook or do anything you need."

Jane's face filled with uncertainty. "We'd love to have your help, Mrs. Roth, but I couldn't have you doing any of the physical work. Perhaps you could read to the patients or write letters for them?"

Cassandra gave a twisted smile. "I'm not precious, Jane. I know how to get my hands dirty."

"Thank you, but I'd have a staff riot on my hands if you did their jobs for them, not to mention a riot from the unions."

Cassandra inclined her head. "Yes, of course." Then she smiled. "I'm happy to take you up on your suggestion."

"Well, that would be acceptable."

Cassandra's enthusiasm bubbled over. "Wonderful! Not only can I be around my father, but also it will be nice to do something productive again."

"Good. Anytime you want to start, just let me know," Jane said, a hint of speculation in her eyes, which made Cassandra decide to be more careful in how she phrased things. It was one thing to know she needed to do something of value, and quite another for others to see she needed it.

Nevertheless, she left with a good feeling, though once in the cab heading back to the city to be collected by Dominic's driver, she could feel her nerves tensing again and her fears returning. Perhaps she should wait a few more weeks, until after Christmas, before speaking to Dominic about the money? But then Jane might give her only so much grace. And what if someone inadvertently contacted Dominic or another member of the family about the outstanding bill?

Her shoulders slumped as quickly as her thoughts, her mind going full circle. She couldn't risk Dominic finding out about Joe. If he learned about her father…if he realized some of her money was going to the nursing home and had been all along…if there was just the slightest hint of him reaching a decision to investigate further…

If. If. If.

If she didn't stop thinking so hard, she was going to go crazy!

Mercifully once she returned home, she had Nicole to keep her busy. She even asked Nesta about babysitting Nicole sometimes during the week, and the housekeeper admitted she'd been fretting about not being able to look after her one-year-old granddaughter a couple of hours a week now that her own daughter had gone back to work. So Cassandra was happy for Nesta to bring her granddaughter here, and they soon came to an agreement that the housekeeper would babysit both infants.

Midafternoon, Cassandra telephoned her sister. Penny and the kids were sick with a stomach bug, so she didn't talk long and promised to call back another time. Her sister hadn't mentioned the marriage to Dominic or her upcoming birthday, but Cassandra understood why Penny hadn't been so talkative.

Yet as she hung up, she had tears in her eyes. Even though she didn't share too many confidences with Penny, all at once she felt like she had no one to turn to. And that was a horrible feeling.

That evening after he came home from work, Dominic played with Nicole then helped feed her and put her to bed. He was so good with the little girl that Cassandra couldn't help but think what a terrific father figure he was for her daughter.

And for any future children they might have together.

The thought warmed her through, then scared the living daylights out of her when she thought about not even being able to keep the child she had now. *Oh, God*.

"How was your dental appointment?" he asked once

they were seated at the dining table and Nesta had served the soup.

Cassandra was prepared for that question. "Not bad, as far as dentists go. I'm having some work done on a tooth that's been aching a bit. It'll probably be quite a few visits," she said, covering herself for a little while longer, but underneath she was beginning to feel a touch of remorse. Another necessary lie. Another guilt trip. Where was it going to end?

His eyes narrowed with suspicion. "What sort of treatment?"

"Painful," she said flippantly, aware of what he was thinking. Did he really think she might take a lover?

He didn't smile. "I'll get you in to my dentist."

"No!" She swallowed. "I mean, I've been going to this guy all my life. I trust him."

He seemed to scrutinize her response, then nodded. "Okay, but let me know if you change your mind."

"I will." She continued eating her soup, but it tasted like drain water now. Could he actually have accepted her comment so easily, or was he just trying to get her to let her guard down? More than likely the latter, she decided. And that meant time was running out for her.

"By the way, Dominic," she said as casually as she could. "My dentist was telling me about them needing someone to do volunteer work at a nursing home where his mother lives." She let that sink in. "I thought it might be a good idea for me to help out a couple of times a week."

His eyes probed, but with a different look in them than a moment ago. "Is Nicole too much for you?"

"Of course not! But that doesn't mean I don't need a break now and then."

His brows jerked together. "You're bored?"

"Not at all, but I will be if I don't keep busy." At least he seemed to be taking this at face value.

"You didn't do volunteer work when you were married to Liam," he pointed out.

"I know. I wish I had," she said, then wanted to bite out her tongue lest he think it was the reason she'd had an affair. "I mean, Liam was always holding parties and entertaining guests. I didn't have time for anything else." She took a breath and hated herself for using Liam's illness like this. "And then he got sick."

Grief flashed in Dominic's eyes for a second, before he had it under control.

There was a pause before he spoke again. "What sort of nursing home?"

He sounded open to the concept and excitement rose in her. "It's for the elderly. And they're seriously short staffed. I'll just be reading to them or writing letters, but I'm told my services would be really appreciated."

"Where is it?"

She kept calm. "In the northern suburbs, about an hour's drive away. I don't mind traveling that far. Your driver can take me," she added to sweeten the deal.

Another pause. "What about Nicole? Shouldn't she be interacting with other infants her own age?"

Her heart softened at his concern. "I've already thought of that." She explained about Nesta's granddaughter. "I think it would be a good idea for her to bring her here for a couple of hours each week. Then Nicole and Emma could spend time together. They're a bit too young to play with each other, but it will still be good for them to have that interaction."

He slowly nodded. "Okay, that all sounds good. Just don't wear yourself out."

His comment wrapped her in warmth, even though she knew he was thinking about Nicole. "I won't."

Right then, Nesta came in with their main course, telling Dominic that his cousin, Logan Roth, wanted him to call him back urgently.

There was a flash of impatience in Dominic's eyes. "I'll take it in the study," he said in a clipped tone, then stood up and strode from the room, his mind clearly on the issue at hand.

Nesta turned to Cassandra and frowned. "Perhaps I should have waited to tell him about the call?"

"It's probably best you didn't. It sounded important."

Nesta looked at the plates of food in her hands. "Do you want to wait until Mr. Roth comes back to eat?"

Cassandra shook her head. "No. He could be a while." She didn't feel at all hungry, but she'd try and eat some of it.

Nesta gave her an approving nod, then hurried back to the kitchen. Cassandra sat there for a few minutes without moving, remembering Liam saying that Logan and Dominic got on well. "Almost like brothers," Liam had said with what she thought was a hint of jealousy.

And now it seemed there was friction between the two men.

If ever she'd needed to be reminded that Dominic could be friend or foe, it was now. If he believed the best thing for Nicole was to shut her mother out of her life, then he would do it.

No hesitation.

Cassandra spent the next day at home, lazing about with Nicole, taking a leisurely bath and generally trying to relax. The bath helped, as it always did, and she felt more at peace now that she knew she had volunteer work ahead of her. She knew she was being a coward in avoiding mentioning the money to Dominic, but talking about money to a man who thought she was a gold digger was paramount to admitting he was right about her.

Yet there was *nothing* for him to be right about.

Then Thursday dawned. It was her birthday and she wasn't going to mention it to anyone. Nor was she going to think about the money. That would be her birthday present to herself.

So after Dominic left for work, Cassandra took Nicole outside for some fresh air and sunshine. She chatted to her daughter as she carried her around the garden beds and stopped to smell the flowers. Then she let Nicole crawl around on the lawn, allowing the sun to do its magic.

After a while Nicole began to get a bit whiny, and Cassandra took her back inside.

"Mrs. Roth," Nesta said as soon as they came through the patio doors. "Mr. Roth telephoned before. He wanted to ask me if I was available to babysit tonight. He said he's taking you out to a party."

Cassandra's heart jumped. Could he know it was her birthday? She could imagine he might have tasked his PA to keep tabs on such things. "Did he say where the party was or what it was about?"

"No. Just that he wanted to give you plenty of time to make yourself beautiful," Nesta said with a smile.

Cassandra managed to say something appropriate, then she took Nicole upstairs to bathe her before her midmorning nap. But she couldn't help wondering. Had Dominic arranged something for her birthday? A family party? She couldn't imagine he would bother, or that his family would want to be involved. Of course, Laura was a stickler for doing the right thing—even though she disliked her daughter-in-law.

After that, Cassandra spent the rest of the day trying not to get her hopes up, but there was still a little piece of her that thought he might have actually arranged something special.

She was dressed in an iris-purple cocktail dress that was stylish but comfortable and was putting the finishing touches to her hair when Dominic walked in the bedroom.

He stood and looked at her, his eyes darkening with desire. "God, you look beautiful."

The breath hitched in her throat. "Thank you."

He looked some more. "I'd kiss you, but I don't want to mess you up."

She hid her surprise—and disappointment. It wasn't like him not to take what he wanted from her lips.

He tilted his head. "There's something about you tonight. You look…keyed up."

"I do?" She didn't mean to be. If he was taking her out for her birthday, she didn't want to spoil the surprise. And if he wasn't…

He tossed his jacket on the bed. "Give me ten minutes." He strode into the bathroom. "I'll meet you downstairs. We're taking the Porsche tonight. The party's not far. It's one of those society things."

Her bubble didn't burst, but it was slowly leaking.

"Sorry about the short notice," he said once they were in the car. "I need to show my face on behalf of the family."

For a moment she wondered if this was merely an excuse to put her off the scent. It all seemed odd to her. "Don't they realize the family is still in mourning?"

"I'm sure they do and I was going to give it a miss, but

now there's a rumor floating around that my father is about to retire."

That surprised her. "Is he?"

"Of course not, and I don't want Dad to hear about it. He's got enough on his mind. I'm convinced it was started by a competitor who thinks he can unsettle our major buyers."

She frowned. "But how can they do that, anyway? Even if Michael retires, you and Adam have excellent reputations and will run the business just as well. I can't see how anything will change."

He gave a small smile. "Thanks for your confidence in us." The smile slipped away. "No, any mention of change unsettles people, and I need to put out the fire tonight. One of our valued customers will be at the party, and I have to assure him that everything is fine. If he was to start looking at taking his business elsewhere, others might follow."

She let that sink in, appreciating the importance of it all and feeling foolish because she'd been focused on a mere birthday party.

Yet disappointment dueled with self-derision. "Oh, I see."

He glanced sideways at her. "What's the matter?"

"Nothing."

"You were beaming before, and now you look down in the mouth."

"Sometimes things get to me," she said by way of an excuse, aware he shot her another look, but hoping he'd put it down to her thinking about Liam.

Thankfully the moment was broken as he slowed down to let the car in front turn into a driveway. And then her bubble finally did burst when he followed, stopping to give their names to the security person at the gates before continuing up the sweeping drive to an illuminated mansion.

Staff opened the car doors for them, precluding Dominic from talking further. Their hosts were a gracious couple who were too well mannered to ask the question in their eyes. She could feel others looking at them and was grateful that Dominic kept her at his side as they moved around the room, his arm around her waist in a protective manner.

Or was that a *possessive* manner?

And why did she feel a little thrill at the thought of him being either?

"Just ignore them," he whispered in her ear.

"Who?" she said unnecessarily.

"All those people who are wondering about us." He didn't need to point out they were probably asking themselves how a woman could marry her late husband's brother within two weeks after his death. "It's none of their business," he added quietly, and then his jaw clenched. "And if anyone says anything to you, please let me know. They won't say it again."

"I don't think they'd dare," she mused, looking at the fierceness in his eyes.

"You think it's funny?"

He looked even more fierce.

"Not at all." And unexpectedly—in spite of everything between them—she couldn't help herself. Her lips twitched. "*You're* being funny."

Surprise showed on his face; then his mouth curved upward in a sexy smile that held his trademark arrogance. "You won't be smiling later tonight," he threatened in a low voice. "You'll be begging."

Her heartbeat began to race. He'd made love to her every night, but tonight would be a special birthday treat to herself.

Just then a waiter interrupted them with the offer to refill their half-filled glasses, but Dominic shook his head and the waiter left.

"Keep smiling at me," Dominic murmured once they were alone again, but she noticed his gaze had briefly darted away from her.

Her pleasure in the moment faltered and died. "We're being watched, aren't we?" *That* was why he was being so charming to her. He was using her. Like Liam had often used her in front of his friends and business acquaintances.

Dominic didn't seem to notice her dismay. "The man I need to speak to is across the room. I want him to see we're at ease with each other. He'll be more likely to believe nothing's amiss with the family if we look sure of ourselves."

She winced inwardly, disappointment biting at her heels, thoughts of making love to Dominic later tonight suddenly not so gratifying. If things were better between them, if the brief connection she sometimes glimpsed between them hadn't vanished again, she could at least have enjoyed some of his company at the party tonight. As it was, right now all she wanted to do was go find a corner to curl up in.

All at once he gave a low curse. "Damn. It looks like he's leaving the room with our host. Paul's probably taking him out to the garage to show him his latest car."

"Then go after him. I'll be fine here." She'd be glad to get away from Dominic's presence, even if it meant standing there by herself. "Go."

He went.

Dominic moved across the room, making sure he didn't look like he was hurrying as he steeled himself to talk to the man ahead. The deep cut and thrust of the business world had always appealed to him, but this time he didn't like it that one client might be able to inflict damage to their business. He hated smoothing the waters like this.

Admittedly, it wouldn't be the end of the Roths—not even close—but they *would* take a hit if Bannon Dale didn't renew his contracts and started furnishing his hotels from other luxury goods department stores. Lost revenue would certainly mean a number of Roth employees, from those who worked in the stores, down to the people in their warehouses, to the drivers who moved the goods, could lose their jobs.

He didn't really expect it would happen, but damage prevention was called for tonight. Bannon had to be assured that Michael Roth wasn't retiring for a long time yet and that no other changes were planned. Bannon Dale Hotels would always get the best from them.

And then he'd have to speak to both his father and Adam about paving the way for when his father did eventually retire. Things *would* change when he took over the business, but he would continue to use his father's philosophy of integrity and fairness.

He saw his target ahead in the hallway. "Good evening, Bannon," he called out, raising his voice just enough to be heard above the party.

Bannon Dale turned, along with the other man, and boomed, "Dominic! I didn't expect you here tonight." He waited for Dominic to get closer, then shook his hand. "How's your father?"

Dominic noted there was more than a gleam of interest in the other man's eyes, and he was glad he'd come tonight. "As switched on as ever and looking forward to coming back to the office next week."

Bannon nodded sympathetically. "Yes, I was sorry to hear about Liam."

"Thank you." Dominic appreciated the words. Then he paused. "Actually, I wonder if I could have a brief word with you in private." He glanced apologetically at their host. "I won't keep him long, Paul."

Paul nodded. "Sure. You can use my study. It's down on the right." Then he looked at Bannon. "I'll be in the garage when you're ready." He left them to it.

Fifteen minutes later Dominic watched Bannon leave the study. He was feeling very pleased now that he'd spoken to the other man. Bannon had heard the false rumor about Michael's retirement and appreciated learning that was all it was. He even mentioned to Dominic that he suspected who'd started it, so he was no fool. Bannon wasn't pleased by the dirty tactics, either.

Dominic was about to leave the study himself when his cell phone rang. It was his mother.

"Dominic…oh. You're there."

"You sound surprised that I answered my own phone," he teased.

"Only because Nesta said you'd gone to a party and I didn't expect you to answer this call."

His brows flattened in a frown. "Is there a problem?"

"Only that I forgot it was Cassandra's birthday today," she said, sending shock through him. "I should have re-membered, but this year has been so…hard."

It was Cassandra's birthday *today?*

Hell.

It took him a few seconds to pull himself together. Then he said, "Okay, thanks for letting me know."

"Can you please give her our birthday wishes? You know I like to do the right thing in these sorts of situations."

Dominic felt a flicker of annoyance. "Don't worry, Mum. Cassandra knows how you feel about her."

There was a slight hesitation. "Thanks, darling."

He disconnected the call and stood there, letting it sink in. Dammit, no wonder Cassandra had looked excited one minute, then the next like the bottom had fallen out of her world. She'd thought he was taking her out for her birthday. He strode to the door and went in search of his wife.

At the party he saw her across the room. She was smiling, and she looked stunningly beautiful. He immediately wanted to lose himself in her.

And then he noticed the couple standing beside her. The woman he didn't recognize. The man he knew instantly. Keith Samuels. Cassandra's ex-lover.

The image of Keith and Cassandra in bed together sent fire spiking through him. He strode across the room, his eyes fixed upon them, anger bubbling inside him. He didn't like the way the other man was leering all over her.

"And I'm sorry we didn't get to Liam's funeral," Keith was saying as he came upon them. "Tanya and I were on our honeymoon. My divorce had only just come through the week before and we'd already paid for and booked the cruise."

"Cassandra, I've been looking for you," Dominic snarled, having to refrain from grabbing the other man's throat as he approached them. Both their heads snapped toward him and both looked uncomfortable.

Or guilty.

"Dominic," Keith said, turning slightly pale. "I didn't know you were there."

"Clearly."

Dominic took Cassandra by the elbow. "Excuse us. I need to speak with *my wife*." He quietly emphasized the last words, then walked her toward the French doors, though he had the sense to make it look as if he was taking her outside for a stroll. He didn't want any newspapers reporting a tiff between them.

"Dominic—" she began. "I—"

"I don't want to hear what you have to say, Cassandra," he hissed, not letting her go until they were in the shadows at the far end of the terrace. "Sorry to interrupt your little dalliance with your lover."

"Dominic, this is ridiculous. There was nothing to interrupt."

"Tell that to someone who might actually believe you."

She flinched. "You make it sound like I met him here on purpose. How could I? I didn't know you were bringing me here tonight."

"No, but you took advantage of it as soon as my back was turned."

"He and his new wife came up to me. I would never have spoken to him otherwise. I dislike the man intensely."

His eyes narrowed. "So you're telling me the affair's over now?"

"There never *was* any affair."

"Liam wouldn't lie over something like that."

"And I would?"

"Your track record isn't so good."

Her shoulders seemed to slump, then as quickly she drew herself up with calm dignity. "Believe what you will, Dominic. I can't stop you."

He wondered if this was a ploy to get some sort of sympathy out of him. It didn't work. Liam had broken down and told him about her affair when he'd mentioned the will. His brother had been on his deathbed. He'd had no reason to lie.

He fixed her with a stare. "You couldn't even tell me it was your birthday, so why would I believe you've started telling me the truth now?"

Her eyes widened. "You know it's my birthday?"

He inclined his head. "My mother phoned before on my cell. She wanted to apologize for not remembering."

"She did?"

"You sound surprised. No doubt she thought it was the correct thing to do."

"Despite hating my guts?" Cassandra's lips twisted. "I'm sure."

He allowed her that small irony. Then he asked, "You didn't think to let me know yourself?"

"It's only a birthday," she dismissed.

He shot her a glare. "You were trying to make me feel bad."

"How can you feel bad when you didn't know?" she said, looking confused. Then she shrugged. "Anyway, it's not important in the scheme of things."

"Not like your affair with Keith is important, right?" he snapped, as everything seemed to squeeze tight inside him. "The affair is over, Cassandra. For good. If I get one whiff of you starting up again, I'll have Nicole taken off you so fast your head will spin."

She took a step back against the balustrade. "Don't say that!"

"I mean it."

She swallowed hard. "I know you do," she whispered, then shuddered, all at once looking totally defeated. "Can we go home now please, Dominic? I'm feeling rather... tired."

With anyone else he would have felt some pity.

He couldn't let himself feel anything.

Not one damn thing.

He put his hand on her arm. "Come on," he said brusquely. "Let's get out of here." He'd had enough, too.

He wanted her as far away from Keith Samuels as humanly possible, but threatening to take a woman's child off her on her birthday had to be the lowest thing he'd ever done.

Eight

The next day was Friday, and Cassandra was anxious to go to the nursing home. She wanted to arrange a start date for her volunteer work. She desperately needed to settle everything so that she could give up the pretense of another dental appointment, otherwise Dominic might get suspicious and think she was going off to meet Keith. He might put a tail on her.

Oh, God, why was life so complicated? she asked herself as she dressed. It was a question she couldn't answer. Not only did she have the never-ending fear that Dominic might take her daughter from her, but seeing Keith again last night at the party had shaken her and was a reminder that she had so much to lose. He hadn't looked the slightest bit repentant about what he'd done to her, and had no qualms about introducing her to his new wife.

At least his new marriage explained why he hadn't been at Liam's funeral. She'd wondered about that at the time, but had been thankful he hadn't graced them with his presence. It would have been too uncomfortable for her. Not that anyone else would have known...except one person.

Dominic had known.

And that had made it worse last night when Dominic had come back into the party just as she'd run into them. Talk about bad timing. And yet, she had nothing to be ashamed about. She hadn't had an affair with Keith.

And Dominic still hadn't believed her.

And he'd threatened to take Nicole from her.

She had to keep reminding herself she was innocent in all this. Keith had kissed her against her will that day, and Lord knows what else he would have been capable of if Liam hadn't come home. Then Keith had twisted it around, not only to excuse himself, but to get back at her for rejecting his advances.

It would *still* be his word against hers. Remembering the sleazy light in his eyes last night, she had no doubt he'd even now perjure himself if brought into court. He may not give a damn now if his ex-wife heard about the so-called affair, but he'd definitely want payment "in kind." He'd have no hesitation in painting her in a bad light. The thought made her sick to her stomach.

She was remembering it all when Nesta called her on the intercom to tell her that Laura Roth was downstairs. Cassandra groaned to herself. She hadn't seen her mother-in-law since last week on her "honeymoon" and she didn't want to see her now, but there was no getting around it. She took a few minutes to put on a calm facade, then made her way down the stairs and entered the living room.

As graceful as ever, Laura turned from looking out the window. "Nesta tells me you're on your way out the door," she said, her voice polite.

Cassandra had to wonder what her mother-in-law was doing here. Had she come to cause trouble while Dominic was at work? She didn't need this right now.

"Yes, I have an appointment this morning." She didn't feel the need to mention the volunteer work.

"I won't stay long." Laura stood there, for once looking slightly ill-at-ease. "Is Nicole taking a nap?"

"Yes. Do you want to look in on her?"

Her face lit up, then fell. "I'd better not. I might wake her up."

There was a lull.

All at once Laura opened her handbag and took out a small gift. "Actually, I just wanted to drop this off for you. It's a birthday present."

Cassandra knew her mother-in-law was only doing what she thought was right. This wasn't about being nice to her. "You didn't have to do that."

Laura stiffened slightly. "Yes, I did. And I must apologize for not remembering yesterday."

In a way, Cassandra wished she hadn't remembered at all. It sounded ungrateful, but she'd rather have no present than one that was grudgingly given for the sake of appearances.

She unwrapped the gift. It was a scarf made from the finest silk in a pretty lavender color. "It's beautiful, thank you." And she meant it.

For a moment, pleasure flashed in Laura's eyes, before she masked it again. "You're welcome."

Catching glimpses of the affection her mother-in-law once had for her was distressful, and Cassandra's heart constricted at the thought of what she'd lost because of Liam. Things were never going to be the same between her and his family ever again. She had to accept that. And she would. She just had to make sure none of this bad feeling affected Nicole.

Something struck her then. Everything that affected her *would* affect Nicole as she grew up. And didn't that mean she owed it to her daughter not to give up so easily? Didn't she have to keep on trying to make some sort of peace with this woman in front of her? And wasn't Christmas the perfect time to make such an effort?

She took a breath. "Laura, I was going to suggest to Dominic that we put up a Christmas tree this Sunday. I'm sure he'd love for you and Michael to be here, too. And Adam."

The older woman looked startled, then her eyes clouded over. "I hadn't thought about Christmas."

Cassandra understood, but said, "It's only eight days away." She paused. "I know. Why don't you all come for dinner on Sunday, as well?"

"Er...I'm not—"

"I think it'll be good for Nicole to have her grandparents involved in her life like this, don't you?" Cassandra said, determined to do this. She remembered her own early childhood—without grandparents.

Laura slowly nodded. "You're right. Nicole needs us here."

That wasn't exactly the response she'd wanted, but Cassandra managed a smile. "Good. I'll speak to Dominic tonight."

After that Laura left, and Cassandra went back upstairs to get her purse. She checked in on Nicole, praying she was doing the right thing by inviting Laura and Michael here, before blowing her sleeping daughter a soft kiss goodbye and leaving.

Then she had Dominic's driver drop her off in the usual place outside the shopping arcade in the city. After

Dominic's threat last night, she was even more uneasy as she looked around to make sure no one was following her. She even went into the dentist's office to make an appointment, then pretended she'd have to check her diary, before leaving and catching a cab to the nursing home. At least now she could truthfully say she'd gone to her dentist.

Her father was in good spirits and that delighted Cassandra. Jane Clyde confirmed that she could start volunteer work there the following Tuesday—in time for their Christmas party. She felt the need to assure the other woman again that the money was on its way, and Jane seemed pleased about it.

So Cassandra felt a little more relaxed when she arrived home. She was sitting on the living-room floor with Nicole and playing with building blocks when her cell phone vibrated in her pocket. Thankfully, it wasn't the nursing home. It was Penny calling from Sydney.

"How is everyone feeling now?" Cassandra asked, happy her sister had called back. Could Penny possibly have remembered her birthday yesterday, after all?

"All better now." A pause came down the line. "Cass, I need a favor."

Cassandra's instincts went on red alert. Her sister was independent and rarely asked for any help, so this must be important.

She pushed herself up and sat on the sofa. "What's the matter, Penny?"

"It's Dave. He lost his job six months ago."

"What! Why didn't you tell me?"

"You had so much on your plate, I couldn't." Another pause. "Cass, he hasn't been able to get another job, and our house payments are behind. If we don't pay two thousand dollars by Monday, we could lose everything."

"Oh, Penny."

"I was wondering if you could lend us the two thousand. Just temporarily, mind you. Dave's got a second job interview next week and it looks promising, but even if he gets the job, it'll be too late to make the payment."

Cassandra's heart sank. She'd help her sister in a heartbeat if she could, but right now was the worst time to ask her for money. She just didn't have any.

"Penny, I haven't got it on me right now," she said, keeping to the truth as much as possible.

"Oh, no!" Penny murmured in dismay.

Cassandra swallowed. She couldn't do this to her sister. "But listen, I'm told that Liam's estate will be finalized by Monday and the money in my account," she fibbed, trying to think fast. She'd get the money somehow. She had to. Even if she had to ask Dominic....

"That would be fantastic," Penny said with relief. "But what if it's not, Cass? We could still lose the house."

Cassandra didn't want Penny worrying more than necessary. "Then I'm sure Dominic will be happy to help out."

"Do you think he would? Oh, thank you! Thank you both!"

"You're welcome, Penny," she said, but her mind was trying to think ahead. Lord, things were getting so out of her control now.

"Everything's okay with you and Dominic, then?" Penny asked, settling down. "When I heard you'd married Liam's brother, I did wonder why."

Cassandra's gaze went to the little girl playing happily in front of her. "It was for Nicole's sake, Penny. Liam wanted her to grow up a Roth, and both Dominic and I decided we would grant his last wish."

"Well, you're lucky the older brother was a hunk, Cass."

Cassandra thought about how handsome Dominic was and how intense he'd been in bed last night. She'd known he'd been trying to erase the memory of Keith Samuels from her mind, but their lovemaking had been nonetheless physically satisfying. Emotionally, they'd been miles apart.

Somehow she tried to sound casual. "Yeah, he's easy on the eyes, isn't he?" she joked, then quickly moved on. "Now give me your bank details, sweetie. The money will be in the account by Monday. I promise."

"Thanks, sis."

"I'm happy to help."

They ended the call, but that was only the beginning of Cassandra's worry. Why-oh-why couldn't Liam's estate be already finalized and the money in her account? Then she wouldn't have to mention a thing to Dominic about any of this.

No such luck.

And then something occurred to her and her heart started to race. This could actually work out for the better. All she had to do was tell Dominic about Penny's predicament, then ask him for a small loan to make the house payment on Monday. That would then give him reason to hurry the money through from Liam's estate, without her looking like she needed it for herself. And he would be none the wiser about the money she needed for the nursing home.

It all made sense. Dominic thought she was a gold digger, so mentioning the money for Penny would be the lesser of two evils. Could it really be so easy?

After Nicole was put to bed and they came downstairs for dinner, Cassandra discovered Nesta had cooked a surprise birthday dinner. The table was beautifully set, and a bottle of champagne sat in an ice bucket on the sideboard.

Oh, heavens, it was the worst time for this. Her mind was in too much turmoil, trying to figure out how best to approach Dominic. Her stomach was jumping with nerves. Yet she knew that if she didn't broach the subject with Dominic tonight, she'd probably worry herself into a nervous breakdown.

Somehow she mustered up a smile, trying to focus on the moment, not on what was ahead. "Nesta, this is lovely," she managed to say, then kissed the housekeeper's cheek. "Thank you."

Nesta smiled with pleasure. "It was nothing, Mrs. Roth. I'm happy to do it for someone like you."

Cassandra was grateful that Dominic walked toward the table right then. She didn't think she could have stood a sardonic look from him on top of all this.

He picked up the bottle of champagne. "Care to join us for a celebratory drink, Nesta?" he said, surprising both women as he popped the bottle.

Nesta actually blushed. "Maybe just a little one."

Soon they were all holding glasses, and he raised his in the air in a toast. "Happy birthday for yesterday, Cassandra."

Their gazes linked, sending her heart skipping all over the place. Hmmm, maybe he wasn't as remote as he wanted her to believe.

"Happy birthday, Mrs. Roth," Nesta said, then took a sip of her champagne.

Cassandra drew her eyes away from him and cleared her throat. "Thank you."

Nesta took another sip, then said, "I'll take this with me, if you don't mind. Otherwise the roast lamb will burn."

Cassandra smiled. "You cooked my favorite meal. Who told you?"

"*You* did, Mrs. Roth, when we were discussing that new restaurant the other day."

"Oh, yes, I remember now," said Cassandra.

Nesta excused herself, then departed in a flash, and Cassandra smiled to herself. The housekeeper was another one who refused to call her by her first name.

"What's the secret?" Dominic asked, coming to hold out her chair for her.

She jolted as she looked at him. "Secret?"

"Why are you smiling?"

Relief raced through her. She'd thought he meant real secrets. "It's just that everyone keeps calling me Mrs. Roth instead of my first name."

He lifted a brow. "Who's everyone?"

She'd been thinking of Jane Clyde, as well. Then she realized this was the opening she needed to sort things out. "Nesta, and everyone at the dentist's office."

He sent her a penetrating look. "That's strange. I thought you'd been going to him all your life?" he said, reminding her that he never forgot a thing.

Her pulse stopped for a moment. Then, "Yes, and that's the bizarre thing. Once I married..." She didn't mention which marriage, "They started calling me Mrs. Roth."

He stared a moment more. "I'm sure you can handle it."

"Of course." She took a sip of her champagne. "By the way, I had my dental appointment today and my treatment isn't as intensive as we thought."

"That's good news," he said, thankfully not looking suspicious of her at all.

Still, she hesitated before she spoke again. "Incidentally,

I spoke to the director of the nursing home and she wants me to start my volunteer job next Tuesday."

One eyebrow lifted. "So soon?"

"Yes. They're very busy with Christmas and are thrilled I'll be there to help out."

He considered her. "You look happy about that."

"Very."

"Then I'm pleased you'll have an interest."

His comment both surprised and comforted her. That was so *not* like Liam. Liam had wanted her at home, ready to be the perfect hostess for their parties, or the perfect wife in public. He hadn't cared that she'd been bored out of her brain with all the meaningless activity. At first she'd even *wanted* to please him, but once he'd shown his true colors, she'd realized she was trapped.

And then he'd gotten sick…

Just then Nesta came back into the room carrying the soup. Once she'd served them and left again, Cassandra decided to put aside the subject of the dentist and the nursing home. The further the distance between those two things and the money she needed to ask about, the better.

"By the way, your mother stopped by this morning," she said, then lifted a corner of the lavender-colored silk at her neck. "She gave me this."

His gaze traveled down over the scarf to her pale pink top she'd matched with cream pants. "It suits you," he said, an appreciative glint in his eyes.

She could feel her cheeks warm. "Thanks. Your mother has good taste." She picked up her spoon. "And I hope you don't mind, but I've invited your parents to dinner on Sunday. Adam, too. I thought we might put up a Christmas tree beforehand. Make it a family event."

He scowled. "What's brought this on?"

"It's for Nicole's sake. She's only little, but I think it's important for her to be around her extended family, don't you?"

All at once his features softened. He acknowledged her comment with a nod. "I couldn't agree more," he said, turning her heart over. "By the way, we've got a Christmas tree from last year around here somewhere. Ask Nesta."

"Yes, she's already told me." She idly began stirring her soup, remembering how Nesta had said one of the gardeners usually decorated the artificial tree each year. It had made Cassandra wistful. She'd never had a real tree, not as a child and not with Liam, who had suffered from hayfever.

"Is there a problem?"

She stopped stirring and glanced at Dominic. "I was thinking about getting a real tree for our first year." No one need know, but it had been a dream of hers for so long now. A silly dream. "It would be nice, don't you think?" She so much wanted this Christmas to be as normal as possible.

He merely nodded. "If that's what you want. Just let Nesta know. She'll arrange it."

He started eating and she did the same, glad he hadn't noticed how sentimental she was being. Having a real tree was such a trivial thing to be concerned about when there was so much else going on in her life, but she didn't want him to know what a sap she really was about this. And perhaps next year they could even go and pick out a tree together. As a family.

He mentioned it to Nesta when she brought in the main meal shortly afterward.

"Mrs. Roth and I have already discussed it, but I think a proper tree would be just the ticket this year." The housekeeper agreed with a smile.

They discussed it some more, then Nesta collected the soup bowls and left. Cassandra was tempted to mention the money, but knew she couldn't spoil the rest of her birthday dinner. She would wait until after they'd finished eating.

It seemed to take ages before they'd eaten their way through the roast lamb and were finishing up with a chocolate cake. Thankfully she was spared a happy birthday sing-along, then Nesta brought in the coffee.

"Everything's tidied up in the kitchen," the housekeeper said, collecting the dirty plates. "I'll just pop the dishwasher on, and then I'm going back to my apartment." She glanced at the few things left on the table. "There's not much here. I'll clean it up in the morning, if you don't mind?"

Dominic nodded. "That's fine, Nesta."

Cassandra's heart had begun to thud now that the moment to talk to Dominic was near, but she managed a smile for the other woman. "It was a delicious meal, Nesta. Thank you so much."

Nesta looked pleased as punch as she left the room and quietly closed the door behind her.

Dominic glanced at Cassandra, his lips twitching with amusement. "Do you think she's telling us we won't be interrupted?"

"She was pretty obvious," Cassandra said, trying not to hyperventilate. She didn't want to be interrupted, either, but for a different reason. She had what she was going to say all worked out.

Taking a calming breath, she lifted the coffeepot, trying to extend the moment, allowing time for Nesta to leave. "Coffee?" she said, hoping he didn't notice her hand shaking a little.

"Thanks. We'll have a brandy afterward."

The brandy would have been better right now.

A double.

"That would be nice," was all she said, then poured the

coffee, and they leaned back in their chairs and drank it in silence for a few seconds.

She couldn't wait any longer.

She placed her cup down on the saucer. "Dominic, do you remember I mentioned my sister?"

He looked surprised. "Yes."

"Well...she needs some money."

His face hardened in an instant. "Really?"

She winced inwardly at his clear disbelief. "Yes." She had to push on. "She'll lose her house unless she pays two thousand dollars by Monday." She swallowed. "So... um...I was wondering if you could lend it to me and I'll put it straight into her bank account." She'd already decided at least that way Penny might accept it as a gift from her, rather than a loan transferred from his account.

"I wondered when you would get down to needing money," he said curtly.

Her heart thudded over at his tone. She actually thought she saw a glint of disappointment in his eyes. "It's not for me. It's for my sister, I swear."

His lips twisted. "Sure it is. That's why you want me to give it to straight to you and not put it in her bank account."

"But—"

"I don't know what you want it for, Cassandra, but you're just going to have to wait until Liam's estate is finalized."

"Dominic, please. You have to believe me."

"I do? Tell me. Why should I believe a woman who has proven herself to be an unfaithful wife and a gold digger? A woman who lies for a living?"

At the unfairness of it, anger rose inside her. She hated perpetuating the myth that she was only about wealth, but all this had been thrust upon her in the first place. She needed to remind him of that.

She lifted her chin. "Nicole and I are entitled to our inheritances, Dominic."

He glared at her. "I haven't forgotten."

"I married you *because* of the money, Dominic. Not *for* it."

"There's a difference?" he scoffed.

"Yes, there is." Their marriage had been about keeping her daughter, even if it was tied into the money she needed for the nursing home. Yet how to explain all that to Dominic without him learning about Joe? If he learned about Joe, then he might learn about her "blackmailing" Liam, and then she could still lose her daughter.

He pushed to his feet. "The lawyers are already working on it," he snapped, and walked out of the room.

Cassandra didn't have time to react, but as she heard Dominic's footsteps go down the hallway, it was the disgust in his voice that made her heart ache with defeat.

A short time later, his Porsche started up and drove away. *Oh, God.* She hated that this raised the hostility even higher between them. But what really threw her was a truth hitting her in the face. A truth she could no longer escape.

She'd fallen in love with her husband.

And he hated her with a passion.

He should have known, Dominic told himself as he gunned his Porsche down the freeway, anger settling like a steel weight in his chest.

Since their wedding he thought he'd managed to understand this part of Cassandra. That she'd felt vulnerable as a child and it had made her crave security…that she was a gold digger who had valid reasons for marrying for money. But there were simply some things too big to ever accept.

And that was all the more disappointing because he knew now she had a depth to her he hadn't suspected before. She wasn't superficial like he'd thought she was. She *was* deep, but of course, that didn't mean her integrity was beyond question.

Obviously.

Hell, he'd come to admire the way she'd survived all that life had thrown at her, but he'd been a fool to forget what she was. She had no hesitation in manipulating him. Sharing her childhood. Telling him she wanted to do volunteer work. *Not* telling him about her birthday. It had to have been for show.

His disappointment tasted like bile.

Dammit, he still didn't understand why she needed to win him over in the first place. She already had his wedding ring on her finger. She already had a Roth child. And now she had him in his bed.

What the hell else could she want from him?

Capitulation?

A declaration of love?

Was she a control freak who had to have every man fall in love with her, and all the better if it was a wealthy husband to twist him around her little finger?

No chance.

She'd be waiting a long time for that. She might think she knew how to manipulate a man, but she was in for one hell of a shock. No one manipulated him and got away with it. Not even the woman who'd mothered his child. At the next off-ramp, he turned the car around and headed back.

At the discovery that she loved Dominic, Cassandra sat in silence for a while after he left, feeling as empty as the coffee cups on the table in front of her. Love had only ever taken what it could from her and left her hurting. It probably wouldn't be any different this time.

She loved Dominic.

And now she had to pretend that she didn't. Could things get any worse than this? It was hard enough knowing he had the upper hand, but now she also had to live with the fear of giving herself away to the man she loved. Certainly he would use it against her if he knew. The Roth men were good at that. Liam certainly had no problem using her love for him to get himself a trophy wife, turning her heart totally against him. She didn't want that to happen with Dominic.

She made a pact to herself then. She would keep her love for Dominic a secret. It would keep her going during the years ahead when he continued to believe she was something she wasn't. After all, she couldn't fool herself into believing it would be any different in six months' time, not even after the letter with the lawyer was destroyed and the threat of Liam's "truth" disappeared.

That letter was the instrument that could take her daughter away from her, but there was still nothing anywhere to prove to Dominic that his wife hadn't married Liam for money or had his child for the money. The proof was there in the money having gone into her account. Sure, she could prove she'd paid the half million to the nursing home for the bond, but that didn't prove to Dominic that she hadn't had Liam's child for her own selfish reasons. Even if she told Dominic about Liam's letter and its contents, it would still be her word against a dead man's, and who was Dominic going to believe? His beloved brother? Or the wife he believed to be a gold digger and an adulteress?

Yet how could she share her life with Dominic and say nothing about Liam paying her to have his baby? Because that *was* true. Liam *had* paid her, except *he'd* been the one to blackmail her, not the other way around. Oh, God, what a mess.

And even after all this she still had to get the money for Penny. She could ask Dominic again, but she knew she wouldn't. Somehow she would find a way. She had to.

And soon.

Knowing her best ideas occurred in the bath, she dragged herself upstairs and ran the water with some bubble bath. Soon she took off her clothes and put her hair up with some pins before lowering herself into the warm suds.

Closing her eyes, she leaned her head back against the end of the bath, letting the scented steam rise up to calm her. It was hard trying to unwind when both fear and love were jumbling around in her heart, when she knew she needed money and she needed it this weekend.

Slow down, she told herself as she mentally forced herself to step back and let her brain relax. If she didn't take it easy, she'd never see the forest for the trees.

Yet she couldn't help thinking how ironic it was that for someone who had supposedly married for money, she had little of value. The only true thing she had of monetary value was an expensive diamond necklace that Liam had bought her, and it had been taken away to be appraised as part of his estate. But she was never going to part with that. It was for Nicole. A keepsake from her father.

At that thought, her eyelids flew open and she sat up. She *did* have something else of value, and it hadn't been taken away for appraisal as it wasn't part of Liam's estate! An antique diamond brooch. It had been passed down from her real great-grandmother through the generations to her mother, and on to her on her mother's death.

Then her shoulders slumped as quickly as the thought came. She'd sworn never to part with it, not just for own sake, but for Nicole's sake now. The Roths would give her daughter so much, but this was the only thing Nicole would have from her side of the family.

No, she would never sell it. Not for a measly two thousand dollars. Not for anything. It was worth ten thousand, or it had been a few years ago when she'd had it appraised. It would still never be enough.

And she still needed the money for Penny.

And for Joe.

Then a thought came to her and hope rose inside her. Couldn't she use the brooch as collateral for a loan with one of those pawnbroker people? She could borrow enough for Penny, plus pay the nursing home back some of the money she owed. Then as soon as Liam's money came through, she'd pay back the loan and get her brooch returned. She wasn't exactly sure how that all worked, but she was certain they had to hold on to the item for a certain period of time.

Yet was she desperate enough to do this? More to the point, was she desperate enough *not* to do it? Her sister would lose her house if she didn't. And surely part-payment would keep Jane Clyde satisfied for now.

First thing tomorrow she would look for a pawnbroker.

At that precise moment the bathroom door opened and Dominic entered the room, startling her, making her jump almost guiltily. She hadn't expected him to return for hours, had even wondered if he would return tonight at all.

He stood there, his eyes hostile. "You didn't love him when you married him, did you?"

She gave a soft gasp, glad the bubbles were covering most of her, not sure where this was coming from. "What do you mean?"

"If you'd loved my brother, you would have insisted on

putting your stamp on that town house. That's what women do." His mouth flattened even more. "*You* didn't."

Her mind cleared. He was referring back to their conversation when he'd admitted the town house was more like Liam than her. And she'd agreed the furnishings had been all chosen by Liam—just like their marriage had all been Liam. Dominic hadn't wanted to hear that then, and she doubted he wanted to hear the truth now.

She tilted her head. "So you still want me to say I didn't love Liam when I married him?"

"Yes," he growled.

"Why, Dominic? Why is it so important I tell you that? You already think I'm about the money. Why do you have to keep challenging me about it?"

"We're going to be married a long time, Cassandra. I don't want to forget what type of person you are."

"Thanks very much," she muttered, flinching inwardly. The situation was hopeless. He would never believe good of her now. She just had to keep remembering that.

Yet there was someone else they had to remember, as well. "What about Nicole?" she reminded him. "You agreed to keep your hostility to yourself."

"And so I will." He paused. "You're not the only one who can playact."

Her breath caught at the pain. It wasn't fair that he thought so badly of her, but better to think the worst of her than ask questions she didn't want answered.

All at once his eyes zeroed in on the tubful of bubbles, then slowly rose up her bare shoulders above the waterline, up her neck, to her face, to her blond hair pinned atop her head.

A hard, sensual look entered in his eyes. "You look good in that."

Despite the antagonistic vibes in the air, her pulse

started to race. "It helps me unwind." And heaven knows, she needed that.

He began to undo his shirt.

"Wh-what are you doing?"

"Joining you." His lips twisted. "I need to unwind, too."

She trembled with expectancy as she watched him strip. Everything came off—and the fully aroused man emerged. She was amazed she had turned him on so quickly, but her own pulse was just as guilty.

He came close and stood erect in front of her. "Move forward," he said, not moving, all taut and masculine. She could have refused, but, Lord, she didn't want to.

She slithered forward on her bottom and he slid down in the water behind her, pulling her back against him, his erection fitting flush against the middle of her lower back.

Their eyes met in the mirrored wall.

"Dominic, I…" She didn't know what she was going to say…just something…anything…to break the moment.

"I don't want to talk," he muttered, his gaze holding hers, his hands gliding up from her hips to cup under her breasts. "If this is all we have between us, I intend to make the best of it."

She wished she had the strength to get up out of the water, but he had begun lightly squeezing her nipples and she could do nothing to protect herself from herself. All she wanted was *him*. He was the man she loved.

She groaned with pleasure. "Dominic, I—"

"Shh, be quiet."

He held her gaze in the mirror like he held her breasts, unrelenting in his possessiveness. He didn't let up as he played with her nipples, making her ache low and deep. Helplessly, she leaned her head back against his shoulder, his gaze holding hers immobile in their reflection. Then his eyes slid downward and so did hers, and they both watched as he teased the rosy peaks through the scented bubbles.

His mouth took on a definite look of male satisfaction as she moaned, and a womanly thrill quaked through her. Then one of his hands traveled lower, searing a path down her belly as if it was on a mission—a search-and-destroy mission to knock down all her defenses. He obviously wanted it all. And was determined to take it.

His fingers found their target and her breath fluttered. She tried not to capitulate too soon, but watching his eyes darken in the mirror as he slicked her up and down under the warm water was tantalizingly erotic. She succumbed.

Only, it wasn't over yet. Once she caught her breath, he started all over again in a domination of her senses that made her glad he didn't know she loved him. He was making her pay for asking about the money. Making her pay in the only way he knew he could get to her. Through her body.

After she came the second time, he helped her out of the bath and dried them both without saying a word. Her legs felt weak, so she was glad she had him to hold on to and steady herself.

Then he swept her up and took her into their bedroom... took her to their bed and sheathed himself with a condom... and took her to even higher heights.

Afterward he gave her a hard kiss before pushing off her. "Now, tell me *that's* about the money," he rasped before he strode back into the bathroom and shut the door behind him.

Nine

Cassandra couldn't believe her luck—if that was what she could call it—when she woke to find a note from Dominic saying he had gone into the office. It was Saturday, so she hadn't expected he would, but it wasn't really surprising. He hadn't come back to bed last night, and she wondered if this was the way it would be from now on. Was their fragile togetherness now a thing of the past?

All because of the money.

Thankfully, Nesta was home and she agreed to babysit. Cassandra made an excuse about wanting to do some personal Christmas shopping, hinting that she wanted to buy something private for Dominic's benefit, but she was more than grateful she didn't have to take Nicole with her.

Unfortunately, Dominic was driving his Porsche, so the only alternative was to catch a cab. She could not risk using Dominic's driver, and she prayed Nesta didn't mention it later. In any case, she'd tell Dominic she hadn't wanted to bother his driver just to go to the local shopping center. As for any personal risk, she'd just have to be extra cautious and keep her wits about her.

An hour later, the pawnbroker assessed the brooch and the appraisal she'd brought with her, glancing at her strangely, making her wonder if he recognized the name. "How much did you want to borrow?" he finally asked.

She held her head high, despite feeling humiliated being in a place like this. "It's worth at least ten thousand dollars, so that's what I'd like to borrow. Ten thousand."

He shook his head. "No can do, I'm afraid. I don't keep that much cash on me." He smiled, showing a gold tooth. "There's some unsavory types about, you know."

Her heart sank. "But that's how much I need. I…want to buy my husband something special for Christmas," she said, then bit her lip, knowing she didn't need to explain anything to this man.

He considered her. "I can loan you five thousand now or you can come back later today." He shrugged. "Or you could try somewhere else."

Doing this again later today was out of the question, and so was racing around town looked for someone with enough cash. Besides, she wanted to keep a low profile and going from pawnbroker to pawnbroker could easily create a stir among them.

She swallowed, feeling more humiliated by the moment. "I'll take the five thousand now." She could still give Penny the two thousand, and pay the nursing home the remaining three.

"Okay, we have a deal. Now, do you have any ID? We'll need to fill out some forms."

She nodded, though handing over her driver's license made her nervous. It was a few years old and it still had her old address on it. "Um…you promise to hold the brooch until I repay the money, don't you?"

"As long as it's within the prescribed time."

"It will be."

She'd make sure it was.

Dominic stood at his office window and looked down at the city view of tree-lined Collins Street below. He'd been working solidly since coming to the office early this morning, trying not to think. He'd often come into work on Saturdays before, but this morning it didn't feel right. Nothing felt right. Of course, he'd never been married before, either. And what was right about his marriage, anyway? What the hell was right about having a wife he couldn't trust or a daughter he couldn't acknowledge?

The phone rang, the caller ID showing the front reception desk. He answered it and heard their doorman's voice telling him that he had someone on the line calling about Mrs. Roth. He wasn't sure whether to put it through to him or not.

Dominic stiffened. "That's okay. I'll take it, Murray."

"Very good, Mr. Roth. Putting it through now."

There was a short silence, then, "Am I speaking to Mr. Dominic Roth?"

"Speaking."

The guy introduced himself as a pawnbroker, then said, "I just wanted to let you know Mrs. Roth left her driver's license behind this morning. I wasn't sure how else to contact her. It has an address on it, but I don't have time to take it there personally."

Dominic scowled. "I don't follow. Why would my wife be at a pawnbroker's?"

"She needed a loan of some money and used an antique brooch as collateral."

A shock wave ran through his body and he only just refrained from swearing out loud and giving too much away. His whole life had been in front of the media. He'd learned not to react. Damn Cassandra!

"What's your address?" was all he could manage as he grabbed a pen.

Half an hour later, Dominic collected Cassandra's driving license from the pawnbroker. "I'll take the brooch, too," he said, pulling out his checkbook.

The guy shook his head. "I'm afraid I can't do that."

Dominic saw what this was about. "Don't worry. I'll repay you the money for the loan *and* a thousand more for your inconvenience. How does that sound?" He started writing the check.

"I'm afraid I still can't do that, Mr. Roth. I have a contract with Mrs. Roth. She'll have to come and collect it herself. I could lose my dealer's license if I hand it over to you."

Dominic stopped writing and gave a cool smile. "I'm glad to see you have integrity," he said somewhat cynically. He wondered how much integrity the guy would have if he *hadn't* been dealing with the Roth family. He rather suspected the man didn't want any attention from the law enforcement authorities. And that worked out well for all concerned.

He put his checkbook away. "Just hold on to that brooch. I'll bring my wife back to pick it up shortly. And I'll still give you an extra thousand for your inconvenience."

The guy's eyes lit up. "I won't let it out of my sight, Mr. Roth."

Dominic took the driver's license and left. He had a knot in his gut. What on earth did Cassandra want five thousand dollars for? No, make that ten thousand. That's what the guy said she'd originally wanted.

It had better be good.

Bloody good.

Cassandra finally made it home again without anyone being the wiser. She'd gone to the bank and deposited the two thousand into Penny's account, and the remaining three into her own account. She'd made an excuse to Nesta about not feeling well to explain why she hadn't bought anything. The housekeeper insisted she go lie down while Nicole was taking a late-morning nap.

Feeling exhausted from all the stress, she was more than willing to withdraw to the sanctuary of her bedroom. She'd left a message for Penny on her answering machine, and was just kicking off her shoes and about to stretch out on the bed when Dominic walked in the room.

And threw her driver's license on the bed!

"I believe this belongs to you," he said tersely.

She gaped. "I don't understand. How did you get it?"

"You left it at the pawnbroker's. The guy called my office on the off chance someone would be there."

"Oh, no." She'd totally forgotten about the license.

"Believe me, I said something a bit stronger than that." He stared at her grimly. "Why, Cassandra? Why do you need money? Don't you have everything you need right here?"

"I—"

"Do you have a gambling problem?"

She gasped. "Gambling problem? I don't know how to gamble."

"You're gambling our marriage," he said pointedly. "And Nicole's future."

She flinched. "Wh-why do you say that? Do you want a divorce?" Was this the way he'd take Nicole?

He made a dismissive gesture. "No, but if we have to

stay married, then I want some semblance of happiness. I don't want to be checking up on you. I want to be able to trust my wife."

She expelled a silent sigh of relief that he hadn't mentioned Nicole again. "You *can* trust me, Dominic."

"Can I?" His eyes challenged her. "Why did you pawn your brooch, then?"

"For my sister."

His jaw clenched. "Don't start that again."

"Why not? It's the truth. Penny needed the money, and I didn't want to tell her that I had none."

He seemed to hesitate. "Is this really the truth?"

"Yes. Penny's husband lost his job. They needed money to make their house payments by Monday or lose the house. I couldn't let that happen." She deliberately didn't say she'd only put in the two thousand, otherwise he'd have to ask why not the full five.

Suspicion furrowed his brow. "So why did you ask for ten thousand?"

She hid her inward gasp. Damn the pawnbroker's big mouth. "I thought I'd take the full worth just in case I needed it before Liam's estate was finalized."

"You won't. You're my wife now. Anything you need, charge to me." He frowned. "Actually, you'll need cash for yourself occasionally, so give me your bank account details and I'll put some money in there for you."

Fear caught in her throat. She didn't want to give him her bank details, or even think about him getting the details elsewhere. It might kick-start him into thinking he should investigate her previous transactions. Clearly he hadn't done that before now, despite knowing Liam had paid her a large monthly allowance, but if he doubted her anytime in the future, what was to stop him? Privacy issues wouldn't matter to him if he suspected anything amiss.

"There's no need to put anything in my account. I'll be fine once Liam's estate is settled."

His face closed up. "I'm still paying you an allowance. You're my wife."

She suddenly realized she could get around this. All she had to do was open a new bank account—and pray that Dominic didn't ever investigate and discover it. Heck, if he investigated her she was a goner, anyway.

She managed to look calm. "Then thank you."

"What does your brother-in-law do?"

The question startled her. "Er…he's a forklift driver."

"I'll make sure he gets a job."

Her eyes widened. "You would?"

"He's family now."

Her heart really began to melt now. He would do that for people he didn't know? "Thank you, Dominic. Thank you so much."

"It's no problem." He paused. "Give me your sister's bank details and I'll transfer the money tonight."

She stared in grateful surprise. How had she thought this man hard-hearted? She had to clear her throat before she could speak. "I've already put the money straight into her account, so thank you for the offer, but it's not needed now."

"Give me her details, anyway. I'll put in some extra."

"You don't have to do that."

"Just give me the details."

"Okay, but I'll repay you as soon as I get money from the estate."

"Keep the money."

"But—"

"Keep it."

She closed her mouth, her mind racing ahead. Thankfully, she still had three thousand to pay the nursing home to hold them at bay.

"Now..." he said. "We have to get your brooch back. I gather it's a family heirloom."

"Yes. It is." He seemed to be waiting for more. "I...er... would never part with it normally, but I knew I'd be able to get it back once I repaid the loan."

There was a pause. "I apologize for not believing you last night."

She inclined her head. "Thank you."

"Come on, I'll drive us. Nesta can mind Nicole." He watched as she put on her shoes. "I see you didn't use my driver. I checked," he added, before she could ask how he knew.

"I caught a cab. But I didn't take Nicole with me," she quickly assured him.

"What did I tell you about—"

"Dominic, it's not like anyone expected me to be going out in a cab, least of all to a local 'Pawnbroker and Money Lender' I'd found online."

"I suppose not." His eyes held hers, a growing admiration in their depths. "You're a good sister," he said brusquely.

Cassandra was pleased, but she couldn't help but wonder. How long would his admiration last if he found out that Liam had paid her to have his baby?

After lunch, Nesta asked if she could have the rest of the weekend off. Her daughter was sick with a migraine, and she needed her to look after the grandchildren. Cassandra assured her that *she* could handle everything, including the delivery of the Christmas tree the next morning.

"But what about the dinner tomorrow night?" Nesta asked, fretting. "I might not be back until late."

"It'll be fine, Nesta. Take as long as you need." An idea flashed through her mind. "Hey, *I* can do the cooking."

"*You?*"

Cassandra almost laughed at the surprise in the housekeeper's voice. "It's been ages since I cooked a meal. It'll be a nice change for me."

In fact, the thought of cooking for her in-laws excited her a little, unlike the dinner parties she'd arranged for Liam. Those dinners hadn't resonated with her like cooking for a family did. And perhaps now this could be a small start to Laura and Michael making peace with her. She could only hope.

But Dominic vetoed the idea that evening as they ate the casserole Nesta had already prepared. "There's no need for you to cook," he argued. "We can organize someone to come in tomorrow night. Even if Nesta's back, she can still have the night off."

"But I *like* cooking," she said with disappointment. She'd already decided on a menu of vegetables with poached salmon and a summer trifle.

"You do?"

She almost laughed. Did everyone think she was incapable of doing any manual work? "Yes, and afterward I'll just throw everything in the dishwasher and leave the rest for Nesta to clean up the next day."

He frowned, then, "Okay, but if Nesta's away longer than this, I'll be phoning the employment agencies."

"Temporarily, right?" she said, hoping he wasn't thinking what she thought he was thinking.

He looked slightly taken aback. "You think I'd fire Nesta because she took some time off?"

"No, I just…" She pulled a face. "All right, so for a moment I *did* think that. And that's your own fault. I can never anticipate what you're going to do next."

His lips twisted wryly. "That's a good one coming from *you*. You're the most contradictory person I know."

"I'll take that as a compliment."

"Will you now?" he said with a surprising dash of humor.

Something lightened inside her. "You expected me *not* to take it as a compliment?" she asked, hearing herself flirting with him.

"I never expect the expected from you," he said, his eyes deepening…darkening…imperceptibly drawing her toward him. Tiny shivers of anticipation rolled down her spine.

And then the oven timer started beeping.

She jumped up, her cheeks growing hot. "That's the peach pie." Twirling away, she hoped he would reach out, pull her into his arms and kiss her, then say, "Hurry back," only he didn't.

And then she heard his cell phone ring, and out of the corner of her eye she saw him getting to his feet. "Can you bring my dessert to the study? I have some overseas calls to make." He didn't wait for her to reply as he strode to the door.

She hurried toward the other door, which led to the kitchen. After she turned off the timer, she stood and wondered what had just happened. Was he having second thoughts about getting too close? One minute he'd looked like he wanted to ravish her, and the next he had detached himself like she hadn't mattered.

And that hurt.

It hurt even more because she loved him.

Giving herself time before she faced him again, she cleaned up, then carried a tray with a piece of the pie and coffee to the study. He was on the telephone and gestured for her to come in while he continued talking. She didn't hang around. She left the tray and went to check on Nicole.

After that she wasn't sure what to do. It was Saturday night and her husband was working and her daughter was sleeping and she was alone. She could watch some television, but that would only give her too much time to think.

Then she remembered her book. She should have finished it by now, but so much had been happening all week that it had left little time for herself. She decided to go sit in the atrium to read among the flowers and plants.

An hour later she looked up and saw Dominic standing a few feet away, holding a small plate with a piece of pie on it. Had he come to join her? Her heart started to race.

"You didn't eat your pie?" he said, carrying the plate over and putting it down on the small table beside her.

The pie was for *her?*

How sweet.

"I wasn't that hungry before," she said, then saw that his sharp eyes missed nothing. He knew why she'd lost her appetite earlier. That he'd shut her out and that had upset her.

He glanced around the atrium. "So this is where you like to hide out?"

"Yes, it's nice and relaxing in here." She closed her book. "Did you want me for something in particular?"

His eyes gave a tiny flicker. "No. I just didn't know where you were, that's all."

Her heart tilted, but not for long, as a tinge of suspicion filled her. "You thought I'd left the house."

He stiffened. "No. It wasn't that at all. I was…worried about you."

"You were?" That surprised her.

"I just wanted to make sure you were fine."

Tenderness ribboned through her. "Thanks," she murmured, perhaps understanding more than he did that he was being protective again. He couldn't help it. It was in his nature.

"I'd better let you get back to your book," he said, seduction clearly *not* on his mind. "I'll be in the gym, doing a workout, if you need me for anything."

Her pulse started to race. She *did* need him for something. Yet she didn't quite know how to tell him she wanted to make love to him. It would make her sound rather... desperate. Or too much in love with him.

"Do you work out often?" she asked, trying to concentrate on the conversation, not his well-toned body.

He looked surprised by the question. "Usually once or twice a week, or sometimes Adam and I play racquetball. The last couple of weeks have been pretty hectic."

She realized he hadn't had any time to himself lately. It had to be hard on him. He must have stresses that needed more than a sexual release.

"I'm really sorry about all this, Dominic. You should be out having a good time on a Saturday night, not stuck at home with me."

His eyes narrowed. "What are you saying? That you *want* me to go out tonight?" His mouth flattened. "Why?"

"No, I'm not saying that." She wrinkled her nose. "It's just, well, you're home tonight because of me and Nicole. We've messed up your life so much. I feel bad about it."

The tension seemed to seep out of him, and an odd softness swept over his face. "I'm not missing out on anything," he said huskily. Then before she knew it, he leaned forward, held her head still and kissed her. It was quick and over before it had begun, but it left the taste of him on her lips. Then he spun around. "I have to go change for that workout," he muttered and walked out of the atrium.

She watched him go, hope rising inside her. Was she beginning to mean more to him than he realized? He'd said that he'd been worried about her when he couldn't find her. He'd said he wasn't missing out on a thing by being married to her.

And he'd brought her a piece of pie.

Ten

A buzzing sound woke Cassandra during the night. For a moment she lay there, trying to wake up properly as she heard Dominic mutter something and get out of bed. He switched on the light.

And suddenly she knew.

She threw back the blankets, but he was closer to her handbag on the chair, and she watched in horror as he grabbed her cell phone and looked at the caller ID.

He frowned then looked at her. "It says Devondale Nursing Home. Is that where you—"

"Oh, no!" She surged off the bed and grabbed the phone from him, knowing something was wrong if they were calling her in the middle of the night.

It was.

Her father had gone missing.

"I'll be there as soon as I can," she told Jane Clyde, then ended the call and faced Dominic, panic rising in her throat. She was going to have to tell him about Joe, but more importantly right now she was scared for her father. "It's my dad. He's missing."

His confused gaze rested on her. "From a nursing home? I thought you said he lived with your sister in Sydney?"

"I did say that, but…" She swallowed hard. "He's in the nursing home here in Melbourne where I do volunteer work. He's gone missing from there."

His brows jerked together, then a pulse started ticking in his jaw. "So it wasn't about doing volunteer work at all? You lied to me about it?"

She winced. "No, it's not like that. I—"

"What else is there that I don't know about you?" he said, cutting her off in disgust.

She understood where he was coming from. She truly did. But she had her reasons. Reasons she couldn't tell him. And she couldn't think beyond the moment.

"It's a long story."

His lips thinned with anger. "Get dressed. You can tell me on the way."

She gave a gasp of surprise. "You're coming with me?"

"What sort of question is that? I'm your husband."

She blinked, then schooled her features. "Er…nothing." She turned away to get dressed. Liam hadn't really been interested in her father. He certainly wouldn't have come with her now.

And Dominic wouldn't be the man she loved if he didn't want to go with her.

Then she remembered Nesta was away. "We'll have to take Nicole with us," she said, not wanting to wake her daughter but having no choice.

Fifteen minutes later Cassandra gave Dominic directions to the nursing home and they were on their way. Thankfully,

Nicole had fallen back to sleep in her car seat before they were even out the drive.

"Now, tell me what this is about," he said once they had left the house behind.

"Joe has dementia, and now he's taken himself off somewhere." Panic swept through her again. "He's out there in the dark somewhere. He has good days and bad days, and he probably doesn't know where he is." Her words caught in her throat. She could barely say the next words. "There's a river nearby."

He reached over and squeezed her knee. "He'll be fine," was all he said before he concentrated on driving without another word.

It was enough for Cassandra, and she managed to blink back tears, grateful she had someone with her for once. At least it was a warm night and not cold.

The nursing home was awash with light when they turned into the drive. Cassandra gasped at the police car parked out front.

Then Jane Clyde came rushing over as Cassandra got out of the car. "They've found him, Cassandra," she said, for once forgetting to call her Mrs. Roth. "Someone saw him walking along the street in his pajamas and had the good sense to call the police."

Cassandra slumped with relief. "Thank God!"

Dominic was out of the car by now, too. He frowned at the administrator. "How did he get out? I'm assuming the place would have been locked up."

Cassandra winced at the hardness of his tone, though she would have asked the same question. "This is my husband," she said to Jane.

"Yes, I know." The other woman pulled back her shoulders, as if facing a firing squad. "Mr. Roth, we think he may have slipped out when one of the staff went out to her car to get something. It probably wasn't intentional that he left. He saw the unlocked door and just walked through it. That's all it would take."

He looked stern. "I certainly hope you're going to look at your procedures and tighten security in future."

"I can assure you it won't happen again, Mr. Roth."

Cassandra watched the two of them measure each other, but she was more interested now in seeing her father. "Can I see him?"

Jane turned to her. "Of course, Mrs. Roth," she said, back to normal. "The doctor's already checked him over, and he's fine. Please go inside."

Cassandra's heart filled with relief when she saw her father sitting on the chair in his room, a blanket wrapped around his shoulders, a cup of tea by his side. The male nurse reassured them of the same thing, then left them alone.

"Oh, Dad," she said, crouching down in front of him and taking hold of his hands. "You shouldn't have left your room."

Her father blinked. "Cassie?"

"Yes, Dad. It's me." She looked up at his beloved face. "Are you okay? Are you in pain anywhere?"

He shook his gray head, but his eyes were confused. "Should I be?"

Her spirits sank. "No, Dad."

He looked behind her at the door. "Liam came to see me, too? And Nicole?"

She glanced behind her and saw Dominic cradling Nicole against his shoulder, watching them. "No, Dad. That's not Liam. That's Liam's brother Dominic."

Her father's face turned mulish. "Good. I don't like Liam."

"Dad," she scolded lightly, feeling herself flush.

Dominic moved forward with Nicole. "Hi, Joe. You've given Cassandra quite a scare."

"I did? Why?"

Cassandra looked at Dominic with despair in her heart, then back at her father. "It's okay, Dad. You're fine now and that's all that matters." She kissed his cheek. "We'll leave you to go to bed. You've had quite an evening. I'll come see you in a few days, okay?"

They took their leave after that, with Jane promising to call if Joe developed any chest infections or illnesses from being outside in the night.

Dominic didn't speak on the way home, but she had no doubt he would once they arrived there. Yet she still couldn't tell him the full story about Liam paying her money to have his baby. Couldn't even hint at it. She had to tread carefully.

So very carefully.

Once home he jerked his head toward the living room. "You go sit in there. I'll put Nicole back to bed."

She did what he said, and all too soon he was back.

He went straight to the bar. "Here. Drink this." He handed her a glass, and she sipped the brandy. It burned going down her throat, steadying her nerves.

Then he sat down on the opposite chair and took a mouthful of his own drink before speaking. "Your father didn't like Liam," he stated, his voice neutral.

She didn't expect that to be the first thing he'd say. "It's amazing how Dad remembers something like that and not other things."

"Did Liam ever visit him?"

She shook her head. "Liam was a sick man himself, remember?"

"I meant before either of them became ill."

Did she shatter his belief about his brother?

"They met a couple of times." She lifted one shoulder. "That's life. Everyone's busy."

He drew his lips in thoughtfully. "I suspect he wouldn't have gone to see Joe in hospital, anyway. He didn't like to be around sick people." He made a harsh sound. "Hell, he hated being sick himself."

Her heart squeezed tight for a moment. "I know." She remembered how he'd hated losing his hair during the treatment, and how he'd insisted on the artificial insemination rather than making love. She'd been grateful for the latter, not because of his illness, but because he'd already killed any love she had for him.

Dominic looked down into his glass; then his eyes lifted. "You didn't really have any dental appointments, did you?"

Her throat went bone dry. "No."

"You went to the nursing home?"

She nodded. "But I was still going to do volunteer work for them, as well."

His eyes snagged hers. "Why, Cassandra? Why keep your father a secret from me?"

She took a shuddering breath. "Because Joe's my father and he's *my* responsibility."

"You're my wife. If you have any problems, you need to share them with me. I want to be able to help."

Her heart turned over. "I appreciate that, but I'm used to doing things on my own. I owe Dad a lot, and I willingly pay him in kind."

"Like you do for your sister?"

She knew he was remembering the money for Penny. "Yes, that, too. I can't abandon either of them when they need me."

He considered her. "Joe's been in there all along, hasn't he? He was never at your sister's."

She nodded. "He became sick when Liam got sick."

"And you shouldered the full responsibility for both men?" His mouth flattened. "You really should have told me about Joe."

Suddenly, she realized he was hurt. This strong man who was always taking on other's responsibilities himself was hurt because she held back from him. Once again she wondered if he was feeling something more for her than he realized.

She couldn't think about that. She had to concentrate on the here and now. And she had to be convincing.

"Dominic, you took on a wife and a child for your brother. I didn't want you to have to take on my family problems, as well." She shrugged. "So I kept it quiet."

He stared at her. "Let me be the judge of what I take on or not," he said brusquely.

A lump welled in her throat. Oh, how she loved this man.

"Do you want to bring Joe here to live?" he asked, taking her by surprise. "We could get round-the-clock nursing, though I'd make the proviso that you not take on too much yourself."

Her eyes widened. "You would do that?"

"Of course."

She cleared her throat. "That's so wonderful of you, but it's not practical. Dad is better off where he is." She sniffed back grateful tears. "But thank you so much for the kind offer."

He stared at her, seeming to jolt. "Christ! I've just realized why you need the money from Liam's estate," he said, sending panic scooting through her. "*You* paid the nursing home fees. *That's* why Liam was giving you such a large allowance. It wasn't all for you, was it?"

Oh, God. He was getting too close.

She moistened her mouth. "I—"

"You said the other night you married me *because* of the money, not for it." He swore low in his throat. "Now I know what you meant."

Everything went blurry, and she quickly looked down at the brandy glass. She couldn't believe it. He'd figured it out, just like she'd thought he would. Would he figure out the rest of it? That Liam had *paid* her to have Nicole? Now was the time when she really *was* vulnerable and unable to trust him, even though every instinct inside her screamed that she should. That was merely her love for him talking. Not her head.

"You really did love Liam when you married him, didn't you?"

"Yes, I did," she said without hesitation.

"I'm sorry, Cassandra. I…" He stopped and cleared his throat. "You'd better go to bed."

"Dominic, I—"

"Please go."

She stood up and left.

After Cassandra left the room, Dominic poured himself another drink, then dropped down on the sofa. He had a lot to think about. He'd been so wrong about his wife. She wasn't a gold digger after all. She'd married his brother because she'd loved Liam, just as she'd said.

And that made him wonder if she'd been unfaithful to Liam at all. Liam had firmly believed it had been the truth, but perhaps there was more to it?

Hell.

She'd been so strong to cope with Liam and his illness, plus her father's stroke and dementia. And she'd shouldered it all alone and without complaint. He could understand why she'd pushed Liam to go home to die those last few months. She'd needed the break. And now she'd taken on her sister's problems. If it hadn't been for the antique brooch episode today and then her father going missing tonight, he'd still be in the dark about everything.

It hadn't been about the money at all.

And if that were the case, could it mean he'd been wrong about the reason she'd had Nicole? Liam had told him she hadn't wanted a child, but had then changed her mind. And that had merely confirmed to him that having Nicole had mainly been about jumping on the gravy train.

That theory had been blown out of the water.

He couldn't deny she was a loving mother to Nicole, a compassionate daughter to Joe and a caring sister to Penny. She'd even remained polite to her parents-in-law in the face of their chilly attitude. She would have been a wonderful wife to Liam, too—if Liam had appreciated her. Somehow he didn't think that had been the case.

As for *their* marriage, she'd only ever been a giving wife toward him. Sure, they'd had their problems but they'd all been caused by his belief that she was fundamentally flawed. Now he knew she wasn't. She was perfect. She had integrity and principles. He was damn proud to have her as his wife.

He was damn proud to love her.

At that moment something very right straightened inside him. He *loved* Cassandra. She was his beautiful wife and the mother of his beautiful daughter, but it was the person she was that he loved.

As soon as Christmas was over, he'd sit her down and tell her the truth about Nicole. It wouldn't be easy, but only then could they start afresh with complete honesty between them. And hopefully then she would listen when he told her he loved her.

* * *

Cassandra didn't remember Dominic coming to bed, but it must have been in the early hours of the morning. The next thing she knew, the sun was shining and Nicole was crying for her breakfast. She went to slip from under the blankets, but Dominic kissed her cheek and whispered, "Go back to sleep," and she did, gratefully.

The next time she woke, she found a note on the bedside table. Dominic had called the nursing home for an update, and her father was fine after his late-night adventure. It was a sweet gesture.

Then she heard a noise and realized it was the vibration from her cell phone. She'd have to remember to put it on sound now that Dominic knew about Joe.

"Cass, thank you *so* much," a delighted Penny said as soon as Cassandra answered.

Cassandra decided not to tell her sister about their father's escapade. Penny had enough to worry about. "So you got the money, then?"

"Yes, and it's such a relief, but I can't believe you put *seven thousand dollars* in our account."

"How much?"

"Seven thousand." Penny sounded cautious now. "Why? Is it a mistake? I see there's two amounts—one for two thousand and one for five thousand. Didn't you mean to put that much in?"

Cassandra was quick to assure her. "Dominic sent the money, not me, so I'm sure it's correct."

She couldn't say she'd put the two thousand in, not after telling Penny yesterday that she had no money at all to give her then. Best to let her sister think that Dominic had put the lot in himself.

"Are you sure?"

"Absolutely." It didn't matter, anyway. The money was in the account now. "If Liam's money had come through in time, I would have done the same thing."

"I know you would, sis," Penny murmured.

Cassandra remembered something else. "Penny, Dominic said he'd help Dave get a job, as well."

"What! Oh, my God, Cass. I'm going to seriously break down here."

Cassandra didn't know whether to laugh or cry. "As Dominic said, you're family."

There was silence as Penny considered that, and Cassandra knew she was gently crying.

Her sister sniffed. "Dominic's so much better for you than Liam."

"I know," Cassandra agreed softly.

Penny sniffed again. "I hope you find love with him, Cass. I really do."

Cassandra swallowed the lump in her throat, unable to tell Penny that she was already in love with her husband. "So do I."

"Tell him thank-you. Or better yet, let me speak to him. I should thank him personally."

"I can't right now. He's downstairs with Nicole." Cassandra was rather relieved Dominic wasn't close by.

"Another time, then."

"Definitely."

They rang off after that; then Cassandra showered and dressed. Downstairs, Dominic and Nicole were nowhere to be seen inside the house, but she found them out on the lawn. Dominic had spread a rug on the grass and was holding a camcorder, taping Nicole playing with her toys.

When Nicole saw her, she dropped her toys and started crawling toward her in her cute little denim jeans and pink

T-shirt. Cassandra scooped up her little angel and cuddled her, her heart swelling with maternal love.

And then she realized Dominic was still recording. She wrinkled her nose. "I hate having my picture taken."

"It's not a picture. It's a video," he said, continuing to record. "I want Nicole to see how beautiful her mother is."

She turned to putty. He'd often told her she was beautiful while they were making love, but not like this. Something had definitely changed between them. Where was his hostility? It was like it had taken a break.

She dragged her gaze away and buried her face in Nicole's hair, biting her tongue. Dominic was making it so difficult for her *not* to tell him she loved him.

If only…

All at once she realized something. After finding out about Joe last night, he clearly didn't believe she was a gold digger any longer. So might he now realize she hadn't been unfaithful to Liam? And could that mean in six months' time she would be in no danger of losing Nicole once that letter with the lawyer was destroyed? That there would be no need to drag Keith Samuels into court to testify against her? That she might actually be able to tell Dominic she loved him?

If she dared risk her heart.

But what if she risked her heart and he didn't feel anything stronger than fondness? What if he *didn't* love her? *Couldn't* love her? Did she want to risk her heart then? She swallowed as her spirits dampened. Perhaps it was a question best answered closer to the time. He no longer had a low opinion of her, and that was a start.

She lifted her face away from Nicole's hair and tried to act nonchalant. "Penny called me just before," she said, watching as he stopped filming. "You put five thousand into her account." She tilted her head. "It wasn't a mistake, was it?"

"No."

"Then thank you." She had to stop herself from saying she would pay him back. This time she would accept his generosity in the spirit it was given. "I told her about the job for her husband, too. You made her cry."

He actually looked a little embarrassed. "I'm glad to help," he said, then looked the other way and jerkily went to turn the camcorder on again.

She was rather bemused by his discomfort. "Let me have that please, Dominic. It's my turn to record you and Nicole together." She smiled. "That way she'll see how handsome her father is, too."

His head reeled back. "Her *father?*"

She empathized with what he was feeling. "Yes, that's how she'll see you. Like I do with Joe. You'll be her father in every way that matters."

He seemed to swallow a lump in his throat. "Yes, of course." But he didn't move.

She was the one to move forward. "Here. You hold her." She swapped Nicole for the camcorder. "How does this thing work?"

He didn't comment. He was looking down at Nicole in his arms, and she suddenly knew the moment was getting to him. She let him have this time.

Then, "How does it work?" she reminded him gently.

Finally he looked up, then blinked as if coming from a long way off. He focused on her. "Right. This is what you do," he began.

Over the next couple of hours, the Christmas tree was delivered and Nicole napped in the shade nearby while they ate a light lunch poolside. Then the little girl woke up and Dominic insisted on feeding her lunch while Cassandra went to prepare the dinner for this evening. Midafternoon, they all had a dip in the pool before eventually it was too much for Nicole again and she started to cry. Soon she had fallen asleep in her crib.

Then Dominic drew Cassandra into their bedroom and made love to her, and afterward she fell asleep curled up against him. If she had to wish for a better belated birthday, she couldn't. She just hoped that tonight's gathering for the family dinner and to put up the Christmas tree wasn't going to spoil things. She wanted everything to be as perfect as possible. So much of that relied on his parents.

Eleven

Cassandra felt nervous a few hours later when Dominic opened the front door to both his parents and his brother Adam. She prayed the evening went well. Goodwill to all men—and women—she added, hoping her in-laws could put aside their feelings for her tonight.

Nicole looked like a little doll in her red reindeer dress. And Dominic looked so very handsome holding the little girl in his arms. She knew she looked quite nice herself, in a sleeveless green dress cinched at the waist with a silver belt, yet it was more about what they looked like as a family. She actually sensed the possibility the three of them could be a real family one day.

If only Laura and Michael would consider her a real part of their family, she thought with a silent sigh. Looking at her mother-in-law's slightly red-rimmed eyes as she kissed Dominic and Nicole, she knew she'd set her hopes too high. There had been no kiss for *her* again. It was obvious she didn't want to be here. Correction—she didn't want *her* to be here.

And then Laura touched Nicole's blond curls in a loving gesture that brought a lump to Cassandra's throat and reminded her how much she valued their love for their granddaughter. It was her one comfort in a trying situation.

"How about we go in the living room and have some iced eggnog?" Dominic suggested.

They all moved farther inside the house, then came to a standstill at the arched entrance to the living room.

"You've got a real tree?" Michael said in mild surprise.

The unadorned Christmas tree took pride of place in a corner of the large room while Christmas carols played softly in the background. It wasn't unusual for people to have a real tree during a hot, summery Christmas, but artificial trees were more the norm these days.

"Yes, I've always wanted a real tree. Do you like it?"

Her father-in-law nodded. "It's a nice touch."

"I think so, too, Dad," Dominic added, winking at her.

Relief spiraled through her. Thank God she'd actually managed to do something right today.

Then Adam slapped his hands together. "Okay, where's this eggnog, then?" he said in typical male fashion. He moved farther into the room.

"My God!" Laura choked, stopping everyone in their tracks and sending Cassandra's stomach plummeting as she spun toward her. "I don't know how you can be so insensitive, Cassandra. Are you trying to remind us that we no longer have our son?"

"Laura, no!" Cassandra exclaimed, hearing Dominic swear, clearly as horrified at the turn of events.

"You did it on purpose. You knew we could never have a real tree because of Liam's hayfever."

Cassandra shook her head. "No! This was about having a living Christmas. I thought it would be a nice touch, that's all. I wasn't trying to cause you more pain."

"You expect me to believe you?" Laura said, her voice clogging with tears.

Cassandra swallowed the despair in her throat. "Yes."

"Mum," Dominic growled. "That's enough."

"Laura, this isn't the time or place," Michael said firmly, putting his hand on his wife's arm.

Laura shook him off. "No, I can't do this any longer, Michael. I really can't." Her gaze returned to her daughter-in-law. "I'm sorry for my attitude, Cassandra, but I can't help it. I know you're married to Dominic now, but..." Her face began to screw up. "It's just that..." She took a deep breath. "You deserted my son. You deserted Liam when he needed you most," she choked, then took another shuddering breath. "And I find that impossible to forgive."

Cassandra gasped.

Dominic swore low in his throat.

Adam muttered, "Mum..." in a warning voice.

At that moment Cassandra decided this wasn't going to work. She'd been crazy to think it might. It was clear her mother-in-law wasn't going to forgive her for something she hadn't done. Michael believed the worst of her, too. So did Adam.

She blinked back tears, then realized she was actually relieved it had been brought out in the open. The time was right to get this off her chest. "Laura, what you said is not true. I didn't desert Liam at all. *He* deserted *us.*"

Laura inhaled sharply. "No, you pushed him out of your

life those last few months. He shouldn't have had to come back home to...to...die."

"But he *wanted* to go home. He *wanted* to be with you and Michael. He didn't want to be with me and Nicole. That's *why* he went home. It wasn't because I pushed him away. That's simply not true."

"How can you say that?" Laura whispered.

"I begged him to stay with me and Nicole, but he wouldn't listen to me. I even asked if we could go live with him at your place. He wouldn't let us."

"No, I don't believe you. He wouldn't do that."

"I'm afraid he did. There were many things about your son you didn't know." She had to tell Laura. "It wasn't easy living with Liam, not before he got sick and certainly not after."

"You were his wife. You're the one who took his love and..." She gave a sob. "You could have helped him through all that. He loved you, Cassandra. You should have helped him, not pushed him away."

Anguish twisted inside Cassandra. "No, I didn't push him away. We'd both fallen out of love long before he got sick, but I stayed with him because I was his wife and because I once loved him. I felt I owed him that. In the end, he didn't want even that from me."

Laura shook her head, clearly determined not to believe her.

Cassandra had known this wasn't going to be easy. "Stop for a moment and look past your grief. Listen to what I'm saying, Laura. Liam knew he was dying. He knew his time was limited. Don't you think he'd have wanted to spend every minute with his wife and daughter? And if not with me, then at least with Nicole?" She paused. "So why didn't he?"

Laura paled a little, but she remained firm. "You wore him down until he gave up and left, that's why."

"No." Cassandra held the other woman's gaze, refusing to accept responsibility for something she hadn't done. She understood why her mother-in-law couldn't let go of the past right now. Laura hurt too much in losing her son, and she needed someone to take that hurt out on.

Her.

"Laura, would *you* have given up on spending the last few months with your son?" She saw the shock on the other woman's face as the words hit home. "No, you didn't, did you?" she said gently.

All at once Laura looked stricken. "But...I don't understand. Why would Liam want a baby so much, then walk away from her in the last few months of his life? It doesn't make sense."

Cassandra exhaled. She was finally getting through. "Everybody reacts differently."

"I know, but..."

"I can only guess he didn't want Nicole to be affected by everything going on with him. I'm sure Liam wanted his daughter, but I think in the end he became too scared to love her." She took a shaky breath. "He knew he was leaving her, you see."

Tears pooled in the other woman's eyes. "Oh, my God, I *do* believe you," she whispered, then spun away and buried her face in her husband's chest.

The relief of being believed was so strong, Cassandra's knees wobbled. Until this moment, Liam had been between them, blocking her mother-in-law from seeing the truth. As painful as it was, Laura had accepted it now.

She felt a hand on her shoulder then, and realized Dominic was steadying her. She looked up at him beside her...with her daughter still in his arms...and suddenly she had to know something. He'd finally believed her last night about her loving Liam when she'd married him. But did he believe her now? Did he believe that she hadn't pushed Liam into going home to die? That she *had* been willing to look after her husband until the end? She needed to know.

"Do *you* believe me, Dominic?"

The question hung in the air. Then, "Yes, Cassandra, I do."

For a moment her heartbeat stuttered as love swelled within her.

And then as quickly a pain-filled looked entered his eyes.

His mouth opened—

Just then, Laura left her husband's arms with a short sob and hugged Cassandra. "I'm *so* sorry for the way I treated you."

Cassandra hugged Laura, but her eyes were on Dominic. She'd seen him give a jolt and his mouth closed, the moment broken. She had the feeling he'd been about to say something to her. Something important. Could it be regret for the way he, too, had treated her?

Disappointed that this would have to wait, she hugged her mother-in-law. "Laura, I understand."

Laura eased back. "But I've been terrible to you. Really terrible. I've even shocked myself at how horrible I've been to you."

"It was your grief talking, Laura. Not you."

Her mother-in-law's face softened. "Thank you, darling. You're such a lovely person. I'm so proud now that you're married to Dominic, and that you've given us such a beautiful granddaughter."

Cassandra's heart rose in her throat. "No, thank *you*

for letting me be a part of your family again," she said huskily.

They smiled at each other.

"Right. Now that's out of the way," Adam said in a joking manner. "Can we please decorate the tree? I'd like to get fed this side of Christmas."

Michael said something lighthearted then, and Laura gave a watery laugh, but Dominic said nothing and Cassandra thought he looked a little strained around the eyes. She wanted to tell him not to worry, that she forgave him, too, but Adam called to him and Dominic turned to follow his brother.

She gestured to the couch. "Why don't you both take a seat," she told her in-laws, "while I go check on dinner?"

"Do you need any help?" Laura asked.

"No thanks. It's all under control." She spun away as the tension from the last few minutes suddenly got the better of her and tears welled in her eyes.

Once in the kitchen she stood for a moment, needing time to herself to absorb everything that had happened this evening. She hadn't let herself admit until a few minutes ago just how much she'd wanted to feel a part of the larger family unit again. A family who shared the day-to-day things like the Roths did. A family who laughed together and, yes, sometimes cried together. A family who shared a *love of family*.

And then she realized her mother-in-law's acknowledgment that *she* hadn't been at fault was a release. She could finally forgive Liam for what he'd done to her, not only during their marriage, but in writing that letter of untruths. She could be generous now. She had so much. She was alive and Liam wasn't. She had their child to love and Liam didn't. And she had the man she loved, as well. So yes, she could be charitable in her thoughts of Liam.

She was on the way back to the living room when she remembered they'd wanted to record the tree being decorated. She veered off to retrieve the camcorder from the study where Dominic had left it earlier.

The camcorder was on the desk, and she quickly picked it up. Then she noticed his briefcase open beside it, and she went to close the lid, thinking he must have been in a hurry and forgot to himself. But as she touched the handle, a heading on some papers in his briefcase jumped out at her. It was Dominic's will.

She didn't mean to look, but she caught her name and she was drawn to see what it said, thrilled to see that he had made his will over to her as his wife. Her heart thudded. He would only do that if he believed she was worthy of his estate.

Then Nicole's name caught her eyes.

And then the wording jumped out at her....

"To my daughter by blood, Nicole Roth, I leave..."

For a split second it was as if someone had unplugged her from a life-support machine. Then her heartbeat kicked back in.

Nicole was *Dominic's* daughter? Dear God in heaven. He couldn't possibly be.... There was no way he was.... Her eyes stared at the paperwork as if it could speak. And maybe it already had. It was telling her that what was in front of her eyes was the truth. *Dominic* was Nicole's real father!

Cassandra sucked in a sharp breath and as quickly shook her head. No! *Liam* had fathered Nicole. He'd decided on artificial insemination because he hadn't wanted to make love due to his illness. Why, they'd even gone to the hospital together for the procedure.

And Dominic had visited Liam.

She remembered now that Liam had said Dominic had

come by when she was being prepped for the procedure. She swallowed back a sob of despair. Liam must have asked Dominic to do this for him. But why, especially after all Liam's talk about leaving something of himself behind? He'd wanted a child, he'd said.

His own child.

No, Dominic's child, she thought in anguish as she started the now seemingly endless walk back to the living room, the will in her hand, her heart in shock.

Once there she stopped in her tracks, her eyes going straight to her baby girl, who was sitting on Laura's lap. Her gaze traveled over Nicole's face with a different mindset now, taking in each of her daughter's features. This was not Liam's child, so there was nothing of Liam in her except by blood as an uncle. An expression she'd thought reminded her of Liam wasn't his. The shape of those little ears, which she'd surmised were so like Liam's, couldn't be. And that smile. How could she have missed it before? It was *Dominic's* smile. God. No wonder he'd been so protective of Nicole.

All at once she started shaking. Her throat seemed to have closed up. How could Dominic have betrayed her like this? How had he been able to look at her day after day and not say anything? That hurt the most. The deceit.

He must have sensed her, because she saw Dominic's head snap up, and then, as if in slow motion, his gaze dropped down to the papers in her hands.

He froze.

He knew.

"Cassandra?" he finally said and went to take a step toward her.

She held up her hand to stop him, then managed to speak. "Why, Dominic?"

He stood still, with a dignity that surprised her. "Because Liam asked me to."

She shook her head, trying to clear it. She couldn't believe this. It was a nightmare. One there was no waking up from.

"What's going on here?" she heard her father-in-law say.

Neither she nor Dominic moved.

"Cassandra? Dominic?" Michael's voice was firmer this time.

Cassandra turned her head toward her in-laws. Her heart broke for them. Not only had they lost their son, but now they'd lost the last connection to that son. How did they tell them?

"You're both as white as sheets," Laura said, concern written on her tear-dried face as she looked from one to the other. "Is everything okay?"

Cassandra's heart dipped inside her chest. No, everything wasn't okay. Not for her, anyway. As for Dominic, sure he was okay. *He* hadn't just found out his daughter had been fathered by someone else.

Before she could speak, Dominic squared his shoulders. "Mum, Dad. I have something to tell you."

A second ticked by, then another.

"Tell us what, son?"

Dominic took a deep breath, swallowed and said, "Nicole's my child. Not Liam's."

All the air seemed to suck from the room.

Then, "Sweet Jesus!" Adam swore from over near the Christmas tree.

"What the hell!" Michael surged to his feet.

Laura stayed where she was, her forehead creased with incomprehension as she looked at her eldest son. "I don't understand," she said, not seeming to take in what he was saying. "Are you saying Cassandra had an affair?"

Cassandra took a step into the room. "No! I would never have cheated on Liam..." she shot Dominic a dark look "...in spite of what anyone else may think." Then her lips twisted. "Of course that didn't apply in reverse. Liam cheated on me, Laura, but not in the way you think. He had Dominic donate his own sperm for the insemination procedure."

"Wh-what?" Laura exclaimed.

Adam swore again as Michael's legs seemed to give way and he sank back down on the couch.

"Listen to me," Dominic said firmly, not moving toward any of then, standing tall. "Liam was worried his sperm would be affected by all the treatments he'd had to endure. At the last minute he asked me to substitute my sperm for his and I couldn't say no. *I'm* Nicole's father."

There was another stunned silence for at least ten seconds, then Laura looked across at Nicole in the playpen. "So she... Nicole is..." She burst into fresh tears.

It was the final straw for Cassandra. She couldn't bear to see the other woman's anguish when she had so much of her own. Dropping the paperwork from her hands, she ran for the stairs, not sure where she was going and not caring right then.

Dominic found Cassandra sitting on the edge of the bed. Sobs racked her body and his heart ached for her. He wanted to go and pull her into his arms, but this once he dared not. She didn't need his comfort right now. She needed to work the shock through her system.

And, dear God, she needed to forgive him.

"Cassandra?"

She jumped up, the lines of her face tensing through her tears. "How could you do such a thing?" she choked out.

Her pain was his pain. "You don't think I've asked myself that question over and over?" he said rawly.

"What sort of man are you, Dominic?"

It was far from a compliment, but he knew he had to take a stance. "You told me you couldn't abandon your family when they needed you. Well, I couldn't abandon Liam. *That's* the sort of man I am."

Her face betrayed a hint of compassion. Then she drew breath. "That protective instinct again, Dominic?" she said sarcastically.

He held himself erect. "Yes."

She took a breath, then let it out, and her eyes filled with confusion. "I still don't understand why Liam wanted you to do this. The doctors had already told him his disease wasn't hereditary."

His insides relaxed a little. She now seemed willing to listen. "In his head he knew that, but at the last moment his heart told him differently." He held up his hand when she went to speak. "And no, he didn't want to back out. Not after he'd asked you to have his baby in the first place. He was concerned for *you,* Cassandra. Not himself."

A hard light entered her eyes. "Was he? Then it was the only time ever."

"I know my brother was no saint but—"

"He accused me of having an affair. He wouldn't believe it wasn't true."

"I realize that now."

No wonder she hadn't seemed to know her way around a bedroom. She hadn't been in too many of them, that's why. Lord, he felt bad for believing Liam now. Whatever the reason that his brother had convinced himself her unfaithfulness was true, *he* shouldn't have accepted it at face value. After all, Liam had told him Cassandra had pushed him out of their home because she hadn't wanted to be around a dying man, and that hadn't been the truth, either.

No, his brother had turned his back on his wife and child when he should have needed them most. All at once he knew why. Liam simply hadn't the fortitude to continue the charade. It had all been too much for him. He had no doubt Liam had loved Cassandra and had loved Nicole as his niece, but in the end loving them hadn't been enough. So Liam had done the only thing he could.

He had given his brother back his daughter.

And had given his brother his wife.

It wasn't what *he* would have done in that position. As sure as hell if *he* had been dying—God forbid—then he'd want to take his last breath in his wife's arms and with his children around him.

"Dominic, I don't think you knew your brother at all," she said, pulling him back to the present, shooting him a glare beneath wet lashes. "But no matter how wrong Liam was in doing what he did, what *you* did was worse, Dominic. I'll never forgive you for this."

Her words hit him where it hurt and intense pain erupted inside him. The only thing he'd been guilty of was loving too much. His brother. His daughter. Now his wife.

All at once he could see everything with clarity. This wasn't just about Nicole being his own child. This was about him and Cassandra. He was standing here, looking at her heart breaking over what he'd done, and he realized it went further than that. He knew then in his heart that she loved him.

And he had to make her admit it…or risk losing her forever.

"That's because it's easier to forgive a dead man," he said.

She gasped. "What do you mean?"

"I mean, you're upset with me because you love me more than you ever loved my brother."

She stiffened. "I never said that."

His heart caught, then released. "I *know*, Cassandra. I *know* deep down that you love me. I *know* because I love you, too."

"Wh-what?"

He knew because it was a feeling of having his heart linked with hers. When she laughed, he laughed. When she cried, he cried. When she loved, he loved. He was aware now that she felt the same for him. It was in her every breath. It was deep in her eyes. He couldn't let this woman go.

"Sweetheart, you give yourself away every time you're in my arms. I just hadn't recognized it until now."

Her eyes went on guard; then she tried to scoff at him. "That's sex, Dominic."

"No, that's love. I'm standing here watching your heart break, and it makes my heart break, too. I love you, Cassandra. I'll never stop loving you."

She stood motionless, the expression on her face telling him she was wrestling with something.

Time ticked by.

All at once she started to walk toward him, and his heart rose in his chest, but then she swerved toward their walk-in closet and disappeared inside, saying, "Stay there for a minute."

Puzzled, he did as she asked.

She was back in no time and came toward him with an envelope in her hand. "Here. Read this."

He took it off her, then looked down. It was the letter

Liam had given him to give to her after his death. "What's this about?"

She held herself stiffly. "Read it and *then* tell me if you still love me."

That sounded ominous, but he knew it didn't matter what was in the letter. He still loved her.

And then he began to read, briefly aware she had gone back to her position near the bed. It took him a minute to put together what Liam was saying. And even then he had to reread the letter.

He looked up with a frown. "Liam says here that he paid you to have his baby?"

She nodded. "That's right. Five hundred thousand dollars." She angled her chin. "Do you still love me now, Dominic?"

He didn't answer that. His love for her wasn't in question. "Why, Cassandra? Why did you need the money?"

She hugged her arms to her body, as if bracing herself. "Why do you think?"

He didn't understand, but said, "I don't believe it was for anything other than a noble reason."

She blinked; then her eyes searched his. "You don't?"

"Everything you've ever done has been to help someone else."

She gave a little sob, and then her throat convulsed. "Thank you for that, Dominic," she said, her voice quavering slightly. "It was to pay to get my father into the nursing home. Liam refused to give me the money unless I had his baby."

He swore. "Why didn't you tell me?"

"You could have used it against me in court and painted me in a bad light. I couldn't let you use it to take Nicole away from me. I couldn't let that happen."

Regret tore at the muscles of his gut. He wasn't sure if

it would have come to that, but his thoughts of her hadn't been kindly not so very long ago.

"Why are you telling me this now? You could have kept quiet about it all."

"Because you wouldn't dare take me to court after what you've done," she said, not gloating, but calling it like it was, making him wince. "And besides, it's time everything came out in the open."

He had to agree there. As much as he hated seeing her anguish, it was a relief to finally give up his secret.

"I'm sorry for hurting you, Cassandra. I really am." Tender warmth filled him. "But despite everything, I can't regret us having Nicole."

Her lips trembled. "Us?"

"She's ours, sweetheart. She's *our* child. *Our* little girl. Nothing will ever change that."

Her eyes clung to his.

"Oh, Dominic," she said and ran into his arms.

He caught her against him…held her to his heart…. Then he kissed her, his lips promising to love, honor, cherish… every day of their lives.

As the kiss slowed down, she pulled back and cupped his face with her hands, loving him with her eyes. "You were right, Dominic. So right. I love you, too. I'll never stop loving you. You're an honorable man, and I'm proud to have you as my husband."

He swallowed the welt in his throat. "Then you're my perfect match. I've never met a more decent person than you."

He had to kiss her again.

He did.

When it ended, they smiled at each and savored the moment.

Then her eyes clouded over. "Your parents must be heartbroken that Nicole isn't Liam's daughter."

His happiness dimmed, then replenished itself as he looked at Cassandra. They would both help his parents come to terms with this, no matter how long it took.

He slipped his arm around her shoulders. "Shall we go downstairs, my love, and make sure they're okay?"

"Good idea." She moistened her lips. "Just give me one more kiss first, darling."

The endearment went straight to his heart as he lowered his head and fully obliged his beautiful, generous wife.

Twelve

Cassandra's joyous heart stumbled when she and Dominic entered the living room and saw the older couple in an embrace by the patio doors. It was clear Michael was lending strength to his wife. Beyond the glass doors, Adam carried Nicole as he took her on a stroll around the garden beds, probably giving his parents some time alone together.

And then she felt Dominic squeeze her hand. She looked at the man she loved, and he gave her a reassuring smile before turning to face them.

"Mum, Dad?"

His parents lifted their heads.

"I hope you can forgive me."

All at once Laura gave a small cry and broke away from her husband. Without hesitation, she held out her arms as she came toward them. "My darling son, there's nothing to forgive. We were shocked at first, but we understand. We really do."

Cassandra released Dominic's hand so he could go to his mother. He stepped forward, and Laura soon reached him, wrapping her arms around his chest, Dominic's body giving a big shudder as his mother held him close. Cassandra's vision blurred as she watched them.

Michael walked up to them more slowly. "You're a hero in our book, son," he said hoarsely and rested his hand on his son's shoulder. "You gave your brother a second lease of life by doing what you did. I don't know what went on in Liam's head later on, but I do know he was thrilled when Cassandra became pregnant. Your mother and I want to thank you for that."

Laura let go of Dominic. "Our son the hero," she agreed, cupping his chin. "Thank you, darling."

Dominic shook his head. "I'm no hero."

Cassandra hadn't thought of it that way before, but they were right. "Yes, Dominic," she said with quiet emphasis, "you *are* a hero."

All three turned to face her; then Laura left Dominic to come and give her a hug. She eased back, her eyes remorseful. "My family has given you nothing but grief, Cassandra. You're being so magnanimous about it all."

She felt a rush of warmth. "I can afford to be, Laura. I have the man I love, and I have our daughter." She hesitated. "About Liam…"

"Shh. You were a good wife to him. I fully believe that now. It just wasn't meant to be." Then Laura stepped back and her glance encompassed Dominic. "I rather think Liam knew you two belong with each other. I'm so proud he gave you both a chance to be together in the end."

Cassandra nodded in agreement. He'd been a sick man, and she couldn't blame him any longer. *Dear Liam, thank you.*

She went to stand beside Dominic, lacing her fingers

through his, loving him with her eyes. Then she thought of something else. "You know, Liam was the one who named Nicole. So now I wonder if it was because it's close to your own name. Dominic, Nic. Nicole, Nic."

Dominic nodded. "I've thought that myself."

"Yes, it makes sense, doesn't it?" she said, looking up at him.

"How lovely," Laura murmured, blinking back tears.

Cassandra turned to smile at her. "Yes, Laura, it is." She had so much to be thankful for now. She shared a gorgeous daughter with her handsome husband, her father was being well looked after, and she had wonderful in-laws who'd opened their hearts to her again. She was so blessed. Liam would be happy for her, she was sure of that now.

"Is everything okay?" They all turned to see Adam standing at the patio doors, somewhat awkwardly holding his ten-month-old niece in his arms, his concerned gaze going from one of them to the other.

Cassandra took a deep breath and put thoughts of Liam in the past—where they now belonged. She smiled at Dominic, then left his side to move toward Adam, her heart suddenly bursting to hold her daughter. "Thank you," she said huskily to her brother-in-law as she lifted Nicole out of his arms, then cuddled her close to her heart.

She took a shuddering breath and looked up. Dominic was still standing there across the room, his heart in his eyes. "Look, sweetie," she murmured, carrying Nicole toward him. "Look who's here. It's your daddy."

They reached him, and as if she understood the importance of the moment, Nicole put her hand out to Dominic. Cassandra's heart overflowed when he grasped his daughter's little fingers and lifted them to his lips, kissing the baby's knuckles.

"Yes, Daddy's here, sweetheart," he murmured. "I'm

always going to be here." He smiled at Cassandra. "For both of you."

Cassandra smiled back through her happy tears. She had her family now, and they were the true family she'd always wanted. And no matter what the future held for them, there was one thing she was certain of. Her family was going to have a wonderful life.

* * * * *

Don't miss the next book from Maxine Sullivan
TAMING HER BILLIONAIRE BOSS
the fourth story in the
DYNASTIES: THE JARRODS
continuity miniseries
Coming October 12, 2010
from Silhouette Desire.

COMING NEXT MONTH

Available July 13, 2010

#2023 THE MILLIONAIRE MEETS HIS MATCH
Kate Carlisle
Man of the Month

#2024 CLAIMING HER BILLION-DOLLAR BIRTHRIGHT
Maureen Child
Dynasties: The Jarrods

#2025 IN TOO DEEP
"Husband Material"—Brenda Jackson
"The Sheikh's Bargained Bride"—Olivia Gates
A Summer for Scandal

#2026 VIRGIN PRINCESS, TYCOON'S TEMPTATION
Michelle Celmer
Royal Seductions

#2027 SEDUCTION ON THE CEO'S TERMS
Charlene Sands
Napa Valley Vows

#2028 THE SECRETARY'S BOSSMAN BARGAIN
Red Garnier

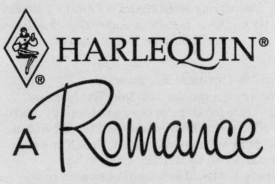

HARLEQUIN®

A *Romance*

FOR EVERY MOOD™

Spotlight on
Heart & Home

Heartwarming romances
where love can happen
right when you least expect it.

See the next page to enjoy a sneak peek
from Silhouette Special Edition®,
a Heart and Home series.

CATHHSSE10

*Introducing MCFARLANE'S PERFECT BRIDE
by* USA TODAY *bestselling author Christine Rimmer,
from Silhouette Special Edition®.*

Entranced. Captivated. Enchanted.

Connor sat across the table from Tori Jones and couldn't help thinking that those words exactly described what effect the small-town schoolteacher had on him. He might as well stop trying to tell himself he wasn't interested. He was powerfully drawn to her.

Clearly, he should have dated more when he was younger.

There had been a couple of other women since Jennifer had walked out on him. But he had never been entranced. Or captivated. Or enchanted.

Until now.

He wanted her—*her,* Tori Jones, in particular. Not just someone suitably attractive and well-bred, as Jennifer had been. Not just someone sophisticated, sexually exciting and discreet, which pretty much described the two women he'd dated after his marriage crashed and burned.

It came to him that he…he *liked* this woman. And that was new to him. He liked her quick wit, her wisdom and her big heart. He liked the passion in her voice when she talked about things she believed in.

He liked *her.* And suddenly it mattered all out of proportion that she might like him, too.

Was he losing it? He couldn't help but wonder. Was he cracking under the strain—of the soured economy, the McFarlane House setbacks, his divorce, the scary changes in his son? Of the changes he'd decided he needed to make in his life and himself?

Strangely, right then, on his first date with Tori Jones, he didn't care if he just might be going over the edge. He was having a great time—having *fun*, of all things—and he didn't want it to end.

Is Connor finally able to admit his feelings to Tori,
and are they reciprocated?
Find out in McFARLANE'S PERFECT BRIDE
by USA TODAY *bestselling author Christine Rimmer.*
Available July 2010,
only from Silhouette Special Edition®.

Copyright © 2010 by Christine Reynolds

SSEEXP0710

Silhouette *Desire*

USA TODAY bestselling author

MAUREEN CHILD

brings you the first
of a six-book miniseries—
Dynasties: The Jarrods

Book one:

CLAIMING HER BILLION-DOLLAR BIRTHRIGHT

Erica Prentice has set out to claim
her billion-dollar inheritance
and the man she loves.

*Available in July
wherever you buy books.*

Always Powerful, Passionate and Provocative.

Visit Silhouette Books at www.eHarlequin.com

SD73037